NIGHTMARES

Damien L Freud

© Copyright 2024 Damien L Freud
All Rights Reserved

CONTENTS

A Normal Day 1

The Seed and the Shaking 6

The Emergence of the Tree 11

First Aberration Encounter 16

First Signs of Global Chaos 21

Early Days of the Research Group 27

The Vagabond's Diary Begins 33

First Signs of Global Madness 39

The Underground Resistance Forms 45

Second Diary Entry 51

Early Research Discoveries 56

Resistance's First Major Strike 61

CHAPTER 13
Tensions in the Research Group 67

CHAPTER 14
Psychological Toll 73

CHAPTER 15
The Vagabond's Diary—Mutating Wildlife.. 79

CHAPTER 16
Desperation Spreads... 84

CHAPTER 17
Underground Resistance—Morality in Conflict.. 90

CHAPTER 18
The Vagabond's Diary—Growing Despair... 96

CHAPTER 19
Inquisition's Involvement 101

CHAPTER 20
Resistance's Major Losses 107

CHAPTER 21
Catastrophic Attack on Research Base.. 113

CHAPTER 22
Preparing for War... 119

CHAPTER 23
The First Assault 125

CHAPTER 24
Fragmented Hope... 131

CHAPTER 25
Beginning the Assault 136

CHAPTER 26
Kellar's Death 142

CHAPTER 27
Discovering the Tree's Weakness... 147

CHAPTER 28
The Last Stand 152

CHAPTER 29
The Fall of the Tree... 157

CHAPTER 30
Pyrrhic Victory... 162

CHAPTER 31
Grieving and Reflection 167

CHAPTER 32
Uncertainty... 172

CHAPTER 33
The Survivors... 177

CHAPTER 34
The New World.. 183

CHAPTER 35
The New Dawn or Eternal Night 188

CHAPTER 1
A Normal Day

The day began like any other, steeped in routine and mundane tasks. The air was warm for mid-September, and the early morning sun cast long, golden streaks across the lawn as the protagonist—let's call him **Isaac**—sipped his coffee on the porch. A small town in a relatively quiet part of the country, his life had always been a steady rhythm of predictability, where nothing much ever happened. And today, Isaac felt, would be no different.

He set the cup down on the worn wood of the porch railing and surveyed his small, neatly kept yard. The grass was due for a trim, and the autumn leaves were beginning to scatter across the lawn. Isaac found something soothing in these small tasks. He had always been a man of simple pleasures, content with the quiet of his life after years spent in the humdrum of city chaos. After the move here five years ago, he had embraced the solitude, the routine, and the quiet charm of the countryside.

He wasn't much of a gardener, but the yard was the one space he allowed himself to experiment with. A few tomato plants grew along the fence, a scraggly rosebush clung to life near the garage, and an old maple tree stood sentinel in the corner, its leaves starting to blush red. Isaac's life mirrored that of his yard—predictable, slow-moving, and, to him, utterly peaceful.

His day off work stretched before him, an open page ready for whatever he chose to write on it. He thought about mowing the lawn, maybe starting on the pile of firewood stacked by the shed. Yet, as he stood there, finishing his coffee, something caught his eye in the corner of the yard—something small, glinting in the early morning light.

At first, he thought it was just a piece of trash, blown in from the wind. But as he approached, it became clear that it wasn't paper or plastic. It was something... stranger.

Isaac crouched down, brushing away a few dry leaves. In the dirt, nestled among the blades of grass, lay a small object—round, no bigger than a walnut, but glowing faintly with an iridescent sheen. It looked almost like a seed, but its surface shimmered in the sunlight, reflecting a spectrum of colors in a way that seemed unnatural.

He frowned and picked it up. The texture was smooth but firm, and it felt unnervingly cool to the touch. Isaac turned it over in his palm, watching as the colors shifted from deep blue to a bright, metallic gold. It was beautiful, but unsettling. He had never seen anything like it.

"Well, what are you?" he muttered, mostly to himself, turning the seed again. It was lighter than he expected, almost hollow, and something about its design—if you could call it that—was too perfect to be natural.

The seed thrummed faintly in his palm, a vibration so subtle that Isaac thought he might be imagining it. He stood there for a moment longer, staring at the strange thing, unsure what to do. Part of him wanted to toss it away, pretend he had never found it, but curiosity gnawed at him. It was too odd, too out of place not to investigate further.

Finally, he slipped the seed into his pocket and decided to think on it later. Maybe it was just an odd type of seed or a prank left by a neighbor's kid. Regardless, he had other things to do today.

Isaac spent the next couple of hours doing his usual Saturday chores— trimming the grass, raking up leaves, and chopping some wood for the fireplace. But no matter how much he tried to focus on the tasks at hand, his mind kept drifting back to the seed. Each time he reached into his pocket, feeling its cool, smooth surface, that faint vibration seemed to grow more noticeable. He couldn't shake the feeling that it was almost… alive.

The hours passed, and by late afternoon, Isaac had grown restless. Something about the day had shifted subtly, as if the air itself was charged with a different energy. The wind picked up, rustling through the trees with a whisper that sounded almost like distant voices. Occasionally, he thought he could hear something else—faint, strange sounds that seemed to linger just at the edge of perception. It wasn't quite a noise, more like a sensation, like the hum of something waiting beneath the surface of the world.

As the sun began to dip below the horizon, Isaac returned to the porch, feeling an unease he couldn't quite explain. He pulled the seed from his pocket again, turning it over in his hands. The colors were brighter now, shifting faster, almost as if the seed was reacting to the fading light.

He stared at it for a long moment, the coolness in his palm now more pronounced. A nagging thought scratched at the back of his mind—**plant it**.

The idea had been gnawing at him ever since he'd found it, but now it felt almost like a compulsion. He didn't want to plant it, not really. Something about the seed felt wrong, unnatural. But at the same time, he couldn't resist the pull, as if some unseen force was gently nudging him to bury it in the earth.

Reluctantly, Isaac fetched a small trowel from the shed and walked back to the corner of the yard, beneath the old maple tree. He hesitated for a moment, staring down at the freshly turned soil. The wind gusted again, and that strange, distant whisper seemed to grow louder, as if urging him on.

Without thinking too much about it, he dug a small hole, just deep enough to cover the seed. He dropped it into the earth and covered it up, patting the soil down with his hands. Almost immediately, the wind stopped. The yard grew still, unnervingly so, as if the entire world was holding its breath.

Isaac stood, brushing the dirt from his hands. He stared at the patch of ground for a few moments, waiting for something to happen. But nothing did. The air remained still, the light fading from the sky as twilight descended. He felt a wave of relief—maybe he was just overthinking it. Maybe it was just a seed, after all.

But as Isaac turned to head back toward the house, a sound stopped him in his tracks—a faint, low hum, coming from the earth beneath his feet. He whipped around, staring at the freshly planted spot. For a moment, nothing happened.

Then, slowly, a small sprout pushed its way through the soil.

Isaac's breath caught in his throat. He watched in stunned silence as the sprout grew at an unnatural speed, unfurling leaves that shimmered with the same iridescent colors as the seed. Within moments, the sprout was a foot tall, its roots digging deeper into the ground, its stalk thickening and twisting in ways that plants didn't normally grow.

His mind raced, trying to make sense of what he was seeing. **This isn't normal. This can't be normal**.

The wind picked up again, stronger this time, whipping through the trees with an almost desperate intensity. The hum grew louder, vibrating through the earth beneath his feet, as if the very ground was alive with some strange, unseen force.

Isaac took a step back, his heart pounding in his chest. The plant continued to grow, its colors shifting and pulsing with an eerie, unnatural glow. It was beautiful, yes, but there was something deeply unsettling about it—a feeling of wrongness that Isaac couldn't shake.

And then, as quickly as it had started, the growth stopped. The plant stood about three feet tall, its leaves glowing softly in the dim light of dusk. The hum faded, leaving behind an eerie silence.

Isaac stared at the plant, his mind buzzing with confusion and fear. He didn't know what he had just witnessed, but one thing was clear—whatever this plant was, it wasn't natural. And it wasn't meant to be here.

He backed away slowly, his eyes never leaving the glowing leaves. He couldn't explain it, but deep down, he knew that planting that seed had changed something. It was as if he had opened a door, and now something strange—something dangerous—was waiting just on the other side.

As the first stars began to appear in the sky, Isaac retreated into his house, locking the door behind him. But even as he sat in the darkness, trying to shake off the unease, he couldn't stop thinking about the plant growing in his yard.

Something had changed. He could feel it.

And it wasn't just in the plant.

CHAPTER 2
The Seed and the Shaking

The house felt quieter than usual that evening, the kind of quiet that presses down on your chest and makes the hairs on the back of your neck stand on end. Isaac sat at his kitchen table, staring out the window toward the yard where the newly planted seed lay buried beneath the soil. He couldn't stop thinking about the strange plant that had sprouted, its iridescent leaves shimmering in the dying light of the day.

He had hoped that retreating inside would help him forget about it, that maybe, in the morning, he'd wake up to find it was all in his head—just a trick of the light, a product of an overactive imagination. But deep down, Isaac knew something was wrong. The air had a weight to it, a kind of thick, oppressive feeling that made it hard to think clearly. And that hum... that low, persistent vibration still echoed faintly in his ears, even though he was now safely inside the house.

He stood up, pacing to the window, peering out into the darkness. The plant wasn't visible from here, but he knew where it was, buried beneath the old maple tree. His yard, once a space of calm, now seemed like a place of quiet danger. The leaves on the maple tree rustled in the wind, but the sound wasn't soothing like it usually was—it felt more like a whisper, as though something unseen was watching, waiting for the right moment to act.

Isaac tried to shake off the feeling. He turned away from the window and busied himself with small tasks—washing dishes, tidying up the counters, anything to distract his mind. But no matter what he did, the unease wouldn't leave him. It lingered like a shadow in the corners of the room.

As the hours ticked by, the unease shifted into something more intense. Isaac's heart began to beat faster for no apparent reason, and the air in the house seemed to grow colder. It wasn't a chill that came from the temperature; it was something else—something that made the world feel just a little bit off.

And then the sound started again, faint at first but unmistakable—the same hum he had heard earlier, the one that seemed to come from the earth itself. It was low and rhythmic, like a distant engine or a heartbeat far underground. Isaac froze, listening, his breath catching in his throat.

The hum grew louder, reverberating through the floorboards beneath his feet. He rushed back to the window, his hands gripping the frame as he peered out into the darkened yard. The wind had picked up, rustling the leaves of the trees in sharp, angry bursts. The shadows seemed deeper now, darker than they had any right to be on a clear night.

And then he saw it.

The ground around the base of the maple tree was moving. At first, it was subtle, just a gentle stirring of the soil. But as Isaac watched, the earth seemed to heave and tremble, as though something was pushing up from beneath. He pressed his forehead to the glass, trying to see more clearly. The plant—the one that had sprouted from the strange seed—was glowing. Its leaves shimmered, casting faint, multicolored light across the ground.

The light pulsed, growing brighter, then dimming, in time with the deep hum that now rattled through Isaac's bones. He stumbled back from the window, his pulse quickening. He knew something was terribly wrong, but he couldn't bring himself to look away.

The ground shook harder, and then, with a sudden jolt, the earth beneath the plant split open. A tremor rocked through the yard, shaking the house and knocking a picture frame off the wall. Isaac grabbed onto the back of a chair to steady himself, his eyes wide with fear. Outside, the plant was growing again—faster this time. The leaves stretched higher, unfurling in twisting, unnatural shapes. The stem thickened, coiling like a serpent toward the sky.

And then, in the distance, the sky itself changed.

The wind stilled, abruptly, as if the world had held its breath. The soft glow of the plant paled in comparison to the eerie red hue creeping into the sky. Isaac's gaze snapped upward, and there, looming high above the horizon, was the full moon. But it wasn't the silver disc he had grown accustomed to seeing on clear nights like this.

It was red.

Blood red.

The color bled across the sky like ink in water, staining the clouds and casting an ominous glow over everything. Isaac had never seen anything like it. The moon hung heavy in the sky, swollen and unnatural, radiating a sickly red light that made the world below seem wrong—like something out of a nightmare.

He stared, unable to move, his mind struggling to comprehend what he was seeing. The hum had grown deafening now, the vibrations shaking the house as if the very earth was crying out in pain. The red light bathed the yard, illuminating the growing plant with a hellish glow. The maple tree's branches twisted in the wind, but they looked wrong now—distorted, as though they had been warped by the force of whatever was happening.

Isaac backed away from the window, his pulse pounding in his ears. His thoughts raced—what had he done? The seed. Planting that seed. He hadn't known, hadn't thought… but now it was clear. This thing—whatever it was—was the cause of all this. The ground shaking, the moon turning red, the unnatural growth in his yard—it all came back to the seed.

His breath came in shallow, panicked gasps as he stumbled into the living room, trying to put distance between himself and the source of the growing catastrophe outside. His mind raced with questions, but there were no answers—only that terrible hum and the vision of the red moon hanging in the sky.

The ground shook again, harder this time, and Isaac heard the sound of glass shattering in the kitchen. A cabinet must have fallen, its contents strewn across the floor, but he didn't care. His heart was pounding too loudly in his chest, fear gnawing at him from all sides. The house groaned as the tremors grew stronger, the windows rattling in their frames.

He grabbed his phone from the coffee table, fingers trembling as he tried to dial, to call someone—anyone. But there was no signal. The bars flickered, then disappeared altogether. He cursed under his breath, throwing the phone down in frustration. He was completely cut off.

Isaac pressed his back against the wall, sinking down to the floor as he stared out the window. The red moon loomed overhead, and the plant in the yard continued its eerie growth, twisting and pulsing as though it were alive, feeding off the chaos that now surrounded it.

The world outside was changing—he could feel it in his bones. Something terrible had been set in motion, something far beyond his understanding. The shaking ground, the blood-red moon, the hum that rattled through the earth—none of it made sense. But it was happening. Right here. Right now.

And he was at the center of it.

For a brief moment, Isaac thought about going outside, about digging up the plant and trying to stop whatever was happening. But the very idea sent a chill down his spine. What if it was too late? What if touching it made things worse?

The house trembled again, more violently this time, and Isaac felt the floor beneath him shift. He scrambled to his feet, heart racing as he backed away from the window, his mind filled with dread. The red moon's light intensified, bathing the room in a crimson hue, casting long, eerie shadows that danced along the walls.

Outside, the plant swayed in the wind, growing taller with every passing second, its iridescent leaves glowing brighter and brighter. It was as if the plant was drawing strength from the moon itself, feeding on the red light, twisting and coiling as it reached for the sky.

Isaac's breath hitched as the ground shook once more, harder than ever. The house groaned under the strain, and he heard the unmistakable sound of something breaking—a window, perhaps. The vibrations seemed to go on forever, growing stronger and more violent, until Isaac was sure the very foundation of his home would give way.

And then, as suddenly as it had started, the shaking stopped.

The hum, the tremors, the eerie glow—they all ceased, leaving behind an unnatural silence. Isaac stood frozen in place, too afraid to move, too afraid to even breathe.

Outside, the blood-red moon still hung in the sky, casting its sinister light over the yard. The plant, now towering over the maple tree, stood still, its glowing leaves flickering softly in the night.

Isaac felt a knot of fear tighten in his chest as he realized something horrible.

This was just the beginning.

CHAPTER 3
The Emergence of the Tree

Isaac hadn't slept. He had tried—tried to calm his racing thoughts and close his eyes, but every time he began to drift off, the images would return: the blood-red moon, the unnatural glow of the plant, the earth shaking beneath his feet. The memories gnawed at him, keeping him restless, anxious.

Morning never truly came. The red hue from the moon remained, casting a hellish glow over everything as if time had frozen in the middle of an endless twilight. The atmosphere was thick with a weight that pressed down on Isaac's chest. He paced through the house, unsure of what to do or where to go. He needed a plan, a way to fix whatever he had set in motion. But what could he do? He was just one man, and this... this was beyond anything he could comprehend.

Through the window, the plant stood still, tall and twisted, but it was far from dormant. There was an eerie energy emanating from it, as if it were waiting, biding its time before something worse happened. And Isaac knew that worse was coming.

By midday, the tremors started again, subtle at first, barely enough to notice. But within minutes, they grew stronger. The kitchen table rattled, dishes clinked in the cupboards, and Isaac braced himself against the counter, feeling the floor vibrate beneath his feet. He ran to the window, and what he saw next made his heart sink.

The plant—the one he had planted just last night—was changing again. Its growth, which had seemed so unnatural before, had now taken on a terrifying pace. The once small, twisting stalk was expanding, thickening, and pushing up higher into the sky. The iridescent leaves pulsed with light, shifting through colors so quickly it was as if the plant were alive, feeding off the energy of the tremors.

Isaac's mind screamed at him to get out, to run, to leave this place far behind. But he couldn't tear his eyes away. The ground around the plant began to bulge and crack as roots, thick and black, burst through the earth. They snaked outward, writhing like tentacles, spreading across the yard and into the street beyond.

He could see it now—this wasn't just a plant anymore. It was something far more sinister. Something that shouldn't exist. A deep, primal fear twisted in his gut, telling him that this thing, this **tree**, was growing faster than anything natural could. And it wasn't stopping.

The tree's trunk shot up, pushing past the height of the maple tree in mere moments. Bark twisted into dark, gnarled shapes, almost as if faces were etched into it, screaming silently into the sky. The branches curled outward, forming long, spindly arms that reached out in all directions. Each branch split and split again, like claws unfurling from a monstrous hand. And the leaves—those cursed, glowing leaves—pulsed with a malevolent energy that seemed to corrupt everything they touched.

Isaac staggered backward, away from the window. His pulse was hammering in his ears, every instinct in his body screaming at him to **run**. But where could he go? The tremors were growing worse, the house groaning under the pressure of the shifting earth. The air had taken on a strange, metallic taste, and the atmosphere felt thick with tension, as if reality itself was on the verge of tearing apart.

Panic seized him, and before he could stop himself, he bolted for the front door. He grabbed his keys, his mind locked on the idea of getting to his truck, driving far, far away from this nightmare. He yanked open the door and stumbled out onto the porch—only to freeze in place.

The world outside had changed. It was subtle at first—small things out of place, like the way the street seemed narrower than it should have been, or how the sky above wasn't the familiar blue but a deep, unsettling shade of crimson. The sun was nowhere to be seen, hidden behind a veil of roiling clouds, and that blood-red glow from the moon still lingered, casting everything in an eerie, distorted light.

But the worst of it—the part that made Isaac's stomach lurch—was the tree.

It had grown far beyond the height of any natural tree, towering into the sky like a dark, skeletal monument. Its massive branches stretched out over the street, casting long, twisting shadows that moved unnervingly in the dim light. The trunk was impossibly thick, its surface rough and scarred, as if it had been there for centuries. But it hadn't been. It had grown in mere hours. And now it was dominating the landscape, warping the very ground around it.

Isaac took a shaky step forward, but his feet wouldn't move the way they should. The ground beneath him felt wrong, like the earth itself was shifting and bending in ways it wasn't supposed to. He stumbled toward the driveway, eyes fixed on his truck, the only hope of escape.

But as he got closer, he realized something horrifying—his truck wasn't where it was supposed to be. The street had warped, twisting in on itself. The truck, once parked just a few feet away, now seemed impossibly far, almost like it had been stretched into the distance. The tree's roots had overtaken the street, curling around the asphalt, splitting it apart. The ground rippled beneath his feet, and every step forward felt like moving through quicksand.

"No, no, no, no..." Isaac muttered under his breath, panic rising in his throat. He broke into a run, desperately trying to reach the truck. But every step only made the distance grow longer, and the reality around him distorted further. The shadows seemed to crawl across the ground, alive and hungry, chasing him as he stumbled forward.

He was so close. The truck's door was just in reach when the tremors returned, stronger than before. The earth heaved beneath him, throwing him off balance. He hit the ground hard, the breath knocked out of him, and for a moment, he lay there, dazed, staring up at the towering branches of the tree that loomed above.

The sky above seemed to ripple, like a stone dropped into water, and the clouds twisted unnaturally. The crimson light intensified, bathing everything in a sickly, unnatural glow. Isaac pushed himself to his feet, his heart pounding as he tried to make sense of what was happening.

Reality itself was warping around the tree. The air seemed thicker, the ground unsteady, as if gravity was shifting in strange, unpredictable ways. The house, the street, even the sky—it all seemed to bend, twisting toward the tree as if drawn to it by some invisible force.

And then, without warning, the tree **moved**.

Isaac watched in horror as the massive trunk groaned and twisted, the branches snapping and shifting as if the tree were alive, aware of him. The roots surged forward, splitting the ground beneath them, creeping toward him with unnatural speed. The earth cracked open around them, creating deep fissures that split the street apart.

Isaac's legs finally obeyed him, and he turned and ran, sprinting back toward the house. He stumbled up the porch steps, heart racing, fear gnawing at every nerve in his body. He slammed the door behind him, locking it, though he knew deep down that a door would do nothing to stop whatever the tree had become.

The house shuddered as the tremors continued, the walls groaning under the strain. He ran to the back window, hoping—praying—that the tree wasn't following him. But when he looked out, he saw something worse.

The yard was gone, swallowed up by the tree's roots. The once-familiar ground had been transformed into a nightmarish landscape of twisted earth and glowing, pulsing plants. And the tree... the tree had grown taller still, its branches reaching far beyond the yard, stretching into the sky like the limbs of some grotesque, ancient creature.

Isaac's breath came in ragged gasps as he stumbled back from the window. His mind was racing, trying to make sense of the impossible things he was seeing. This wasn't real. It couldn't be real.

But it **was**.

He could feel the wrongness of it in his bones, in the air he breathed. Reality itself was warping, bending to the will of the tree, and Isaac was trapped in the middle of it. There was no escaping this. Not now. Not anymore.

He backed into the living room, the floor beneath him trembling with each step. The shadows cast by the red light seemed to stretch and writhe, twisting in ways that defied logic. He could hear the creaking of the tree outside, growing louder, more insistent. It was alive—more than alive. It was watching him. And somehow, it was coming for him.

Isaac sank to the floor, his back against the wall, his heart pounding in his chest. There was nowhere left to run. The tree had him now. And it wasn't letting go.

CHAPTER 4
First Aberration Encounter

Isaac sat trembling on the floor, his back pressed against the cold wall, trying to steady his breath. He could still hear the deep groan of the tree outside, its massive roots splitting the earth, sending tremors through the house. His mind raced, struggling to comprehend the impossible things he had seen: the tree's rapid, monstrous growth, the warped reality that seemed to stretch and bend around it, and the sickening red light that clung to the sky like a curse.

His gaze darted toward the window, but he couldn't bring himself to look outside again. Something was happening—something far worse than he could have imagined. He could feel it in the air, that ominous tension, the quiet before a storm. A part of him wanted to hide, to wait this out and hope it would pass. But another part—the more terrified, primal part—knew that something far worse was yet to come.

And then, it happened.

The sound was faint at first, like the crack of a twig in the distance. Isaac froze, every muscle tensing as he strained to listen. The sound came again, louder this time—**a sharp, snapping noise**, followed by a wet, slithering sound that sent chills down his spine. He turned his head slowly, his eyes drawn toward the yard as if pulled by some unseen force.

The shadows outside were shifting, moving unnaturally, as if the yard had become a living thing. But it wasn't the shadows that held his attention. It was something else—something emerging from the base of the tree.

Isaac pushed himself up, his legs shaky, and crept toward the window, his heart hammering in his chest. He didn't want to look. Every instinct screamed at him to run, to hide, to do anything but confront whatever was out there. But he couldn't stop himself. He had to know.

Peering out from the edge of the window, Isaac saw it.

The tree's thick, twisted trunk was covered in large, bulbous growths—dark cocoons that pulsed with a faint, sickly glow. They had been there before, unnoticed in the chaos of the tree's rapid expansion. But now, one of them was cracking open.

His stomach turned as he watched the cocoon split down the middle, a thick, black ooze seeping from the cracks. The air around it shimmered, distorting as the cocoon continued to break apart, revealing something inside. Isaac's breath caught in his throat. He couldn't look away.

At first, all he saw was an indistinct mass, writhing and twitching as it emerged from the cocoon. Then, as the ooze dripped away, it took shape—a grotesque, twisted form that shouldn't have existed in any reality Isaac had ever known.

It was a creature made almost entirely of eyes.

Dozens of eyes, all different sizes, clustered together in a nightmarish jumble, connected by slick, sinewy tendrils that pulsed with each beat of some unseen heart. The creature's body writhed as it fully broke free from the cocoon, its eyes blinking in unison, turning, scanning its surroundings. Each eye moved independently, swiveling in all directions, as if searching, as if **hungry**.

Isaac's heart pounded in his chest. He backed away from the window, terror gripping him, but he couldn't tear his gaze away from the creature. It didn't walk; instead, it slithered, its grotesque form undulating as it pulled itself across the yard with its tendrils, leaving behind a trail of viscous black ooze. The eyes—there were so many of them, all moving, all blinking—locked onto Isaac's house.

For a moment, Isaac stood frozen in place. He felt his breath catch in his throat as the creature's many eyes fixated on him. It was impossible to tell whether the thing saw him through the window, or whether it could even comprehend his presence. But then one of the larger eyes—its iris a swirling mass of sickening green and yellow—stared straight into the window.

Straight at him.

Isaac's blood turned to ice. He stumbled backward, his feet catching on the edge of the coffee table, and he crashed to the floor with a thud. Pain shot through his shoulder, but the shock of it wasn't enough to break through the overwhelming terror that now consumed him.

The creature moved faster now, slithering across the yard, its mass of eyes fixated on the house. It was coming for him.

Isaac scrambled to his feet, his mind racing for a way out. He had to leave—he couldn't stay here, not with that **thing** outside. The truck. He needed to get to his truck. But the last time he had tried, the street had warped into a distorted maze, his truck impossibly far out of reach. Could he even get to it now? Did he have any other choice?

Another loud crack echoed from the yard. Isaac whipped his head around just in time to see another cocoon splitting open. **Another creature**—this one even larger—was forcing its way free, its body slick and glistening with the same black ooze. More eyes, more tendrils, more impossible, twisted life.

He bolted for the back door, his breath coming in ragged gasps. His fingers fumbled with the lock, but he managed to yank the door open and stumbled out into the yard. The night air was thick and heavy, the red glow from the sky casting long, distorted shadows that seemed to move of their own accord. The ground beneath his feet felt unstable, as if it were shifting, warping with every step.

Behind him, the creatures moved closer. Isaac could hear them—**that slithering, wet sound** that made his stomach churn. The air around them seemed to ripple, distorting like heatwaves, warping the very reality around them.

Isaac ran. He sprinted across the yard, his eyes locked on the twisted tree at the center of it all. The ground shifted beneath him, cracks splitting the earth as roots burst forth, trying to trip him, trying to pull him back. The roots were alive, grasping at his feet like serpents, curling around his ankles, trying to drag him down into the earth.

But Isaac pushed forward, adrenaline surging through his veins. He reached the far side of the yard, just beyond the reach of the creature's tendrils. For a brief moment, he thought he might make it—thought he could escape, get to the street, find some way out of this nightmare.

But then the ground itself seemed to betray him. The earth shifted again, harder this time, sending him sprawling to the ground. His hands scraped against the dirt as he struggled to push himself up, but before he could move, one of the creature's tendrils wrapped around his ankle, pulling him back.

Isaac screamed, kicking frantically, but the tendril held fast, its grip cold and slimy. The creature dragged him backward, inch by inch, toward the twisted, glowing mass of the tree. His hands clawed at the dirt, trying to find some purchase, but it was no use. The thing was too strong.

As it pulled him closer, the other creature—the one that had emerged second—slithered into view, its mass of eyes blinking in unison as it approached. The eyes swiveled, focusing on Isaac, and for a moment, he felt like prey being stalked by some ancient, hungry predator.

Isaac's vision blurred, panic overwhelming him. His breath came in ragged gasps as the world twisted and warped around him. The red light from the moon grew more intense, casting everything in a grotesque, nightmarish hue.

He couldn't think, couldn't breathe. All he knew was that he had to get away.

With one last desperate surge of energy, Isaac kicked out at the tendril wrapped around his ankle. He twisted his body, ignoring the searing pain in his leg, and managed to wrench himself free. He scrambled to his feet, barely able to keep his balance on the unstable ground, and ran.

He didn't know where he was going—he just knew he had to move, had to get away from the creatures, from the tree, from this nightmare that had become his reality.

The air was thick with the sound of their slithering, wet movements behind him, but Isaac didn't look back. He ran blindly through the yard, past the twisting, writhing roots, past the glowing, unnatural leaves, until he reached the back fence. Without thinking, he climbed, throwing himself over the fence and landing hard on the other side.

He lay there for a moment, panting, his body shaking with exhaustion and fear. The sounds of the creatures were distant now, muffled by the thick walls of the yard, but he knew they were still out there. Waiting.

Isaac forced himself to his feet, his legs trembling beneath him. He had no idea what had just happened, no idea what those things were or how any of this was possible.

First Signs of Global Chaos

Isaac sat in his living room, staring blankly at the screen of his laptop, his mind far removed from anything that could be called normal. Outside, the blood-red sky had not changed. The tree loomed over the yard, its grotesque branches twisting ever upward, casting long, creeping shadows that seemed to pulse with malevolent energy. Every now and then, Isaac would hear the distant sound of shifting earth or the unsettling crack of another cocoon splitting open.

He hadn't ventured outside since the night the first aberration had appeared. He didn't want to know what other horrors had crawled free from those dark, oozing cocoons. But staying inside did little to quiet his mind, and he felt trapped, caught in an ever-tightening web of fear and confusion. His house was no longer a refuge; it was a cage, holding him in place while something unimaginable took root outside.

Isaac turned his gaze back to the laptop screen. He had been combing through news reports for hours, hoping for some kind of explanation—something that could make sense of the madness unfolding around him. But what he found only deepened his fear.

The chaos wasn't just confined to his small town. The tree, and the strange phenomena it brought with it, had begun to appear all over the world.

First Reports of Global Chaos

It had started with vague, fragmented reports—strange weather patterns, unusual plant growths, minor earthquakes. But soon, the news became impossible to ignore. Images and videos began to surface, showing trees just like the one in Isaac's yard, bursting from the ground in cities and towns across the globe. They grew at an unnatural pace, towering over buildings, their twisted branches stretching into the sky. And everywhere they appeared, reality began to warp.

Isaac clicked through one report after another, watching footage from cities he had never been to but now felt connected to by the shared horror. In Tokyo, a tree had erupted in the middle of a densely populated district. The footage showed buildings cracking and crumbling as thick roots tore through the streets. People ran in all directions, their screams drowned out by the deep, unnatural hum that seemed to accompany every new tree.

In Berlin, residents reported strange electrical phenomena—streetlights flickered erratically, and electronic devices malfunctioned, as if reality itself was short-circuiting. Footage showed glowing plants sprouting from the sidewalks, their leaves shimmering with the same iridescent glow Isaac had seen in his own yard. The air around the trees seemed to warp, like the heat waves that rise off a summer road, but thicker, more solid—distorting everything around them.

In São Paulo, another tree had emerged in the heart of the city. Massive tendrils wrapped around skyscrapers, pulling them down as though the trees were devouring the very landscape. Reports described the atmosphere as suffocating, heavy with the same oppressive tension Isaac had felt in the moments before the ground had shaken in his yard. People there spoke of hallucinations—visions of strange creatures and distorted worlds that flickered at the edges of their perception.

In New York, it was worse. A tree had erupted in Central Park, sending shockwaves through the city. The footage was the most disturbing yet—buildings cracked and twisted as though being pulled into a vortex, their very foundations warping under the tree's influence. Streets collapsed into sinkholes as thick roots tore through the asphalt. Isaac watched in horror as a massive branch pierced through the side of an office building, the structure collapsing in on itself as if it were made of paper. The camera feed cut to black as the building crumbled to the ground.

The most chilling reports, however, came from the people who lived closest to these trees. Some spoke of hearing whispers in the night—soft, unsettling voices that seemed to come from the trees themselves. Others described seeing creatures—twisted, monstrous forms—moving through the shadows, lurking at the edge of their vision. There were reports of people disappearing without a trace, entire neighborhoods being overtaken by the trees' expanding roots.

Isaac's blood ran cold as he clicked through these reports, realizing that the nightmare he was living wasn't just his own—it was spreading. The world was unraveling, and no one seemed to know how to stop it.

The Research Group

Amidst the chaos, a group of scientists had begun to investigate. The reports referred to them as the **Global Research Initiative on Anomalous Phenomena (GRIAP)**, a team of international experts assembled by various governments and scientific organizations. They were tasked with studying the sudden appearance of the trees and the strange phenomena surrounding them.

Isaac scrolled through a video that introduced some of the members of the group. Dr. Isabel Martinez, a leading botanist from Brazil, appeared on screen, standing in front of what looked like an underground laboratory. She spoke with a calm determination, explaining how her team had begun to study the trees' effects on the local environment. Next to her was Dr. David Johansson, a physicist from Sweden, who theorized that the trees were warping spacetime itself. His grim expression did nothing to ease Isaac's growing sense of dread.

The GRIAP team had been studying these phenomena since the first tree appeared—long before the public had even begun to notice. Their research had initially focused on the rapid growth of the trees and the effects they had on the environment. Dr. Martinez explained how the trees' roots were spreading faster than they should be able to, breaking apart soil and rock with ease. The plants and animals in the surrounding areas had begun to mutate, developing new traits and behaviors that defied explanation.

"We believe these trees are connected to something much larger," Dr. Johansson said in one interview, his voice low and serious. "The laws of physics as we understand them are being disrupted in the vicinity of these trees. We're seeing gravitational anomalies, electromagnetic distortions, and changes in the fabric of reality itself."

Isaac's stomach churned as he listened to them describe the things he had experienced firsthand. The warping of reality, the strange atmospheric tension, the feeling that something was deeply, fundamentally wrong—he had lived through it all. But even as these scientists described their findings, there was one thing they couldn't explain.

What had caused this?

Dr. Martinez and her team had collected samples of the soil and air around the trees, trying to analyze the biochemical properties that might explain the trees' rapid growth. But every time they sent teams out into the field, their data was incomplete. Equipment malfunctioned, samples were corrupted, and in some cases, entire expeditions disappeared without a trace.

Despite the growing danger, GRIAP continued their work. Dr. Martinez described how they had set up a series of experiments to track the trees' growth patterns, monitoring how the trees interacted with the environment. One video showed a drone hovering over one of the trees, capturing footage of its roots spreading underground. But as the drone approached the tree, the feed cut to static, and the video ended abruptly.

"The trees seem to emit some kind of energy field," Dr. Martinez explained in a later report. "We're not sure what it is yet, but it interferes with our equipment—especially anything electronic. We've lost several drones trying to get close enough to collect meaningful data."

In another report, Dr. Johansson spoke about the effects the trees were having on time itself. "We've seen evidence of time dilation near the trees," he said. "In some cases, it appears as though time slows down, while in others, it speeds up. We've even had instances where teams have reported losing hours, only to find that they had only been gone a few minutes."

The footage cut to an image of a research team in hazmat suits, standing at the edge of a large crater where a tree had recently emerged. They were collecting soil samples, their movements cautious and deliberate. The air around them shimmered, as if reality itself was bending.

Isaac watched in numb disbelief. The world he knew was falling apart. The trees weren't just growing—they were changing everything around them, warping the very fabric of existence.

The Spread of Fear

It wasn't just the physical destruction that terrified Isaac. It was the growing sense of helplessness. Governments had tried to contain the trees, cordoning off affected areas and evacuating civilians. But the trees were spreading too fast. Every day, new reports came in of cities overtaken, of strange creatures appearing in the shadows, of people disappearing without a trace.

No one knew how to fight it.

Isaac closed the laptop, his mind reeling from the flood of information. What he had experienced was part of something much larger—something global. The trees were spreading, changing the world in ways no one could fully understand. And the worst part was, it wasn't just a natural disaster. It was something more—something **intelligent**. The trees seemed to be aware, growing in ways that defied logic, warping reality to their will.

The hum of the tree outside grew louder again, a deep, resonant vibration that seemed to sink into Isaac's bones. He stood up, his legs shaky, and moved to the window. The tree loomed larger than ever, its branches twisting in ways that made his head hurt to look at. The air around it shimmered, bending, distorting.

He couldn't stay here. He had to get out. But where could he go? The world outside was changing, and nowhere seemed safe anymore.

The first signs of global chaos were everywhere. And Isaac had a sickening feeling that things were only going to get worse.

Early Days of the Research Group

In early 2024, as reports of the strange, rapidly growing trees began to flood in from across the globe, governments scrambled to make sense of the emerging threat. The world was still trying to understand what had triggered this bizarre and unnatural phenomenon. The first trees had appeared seemingly overnight, tearing through urban landscapes, forests, and deserts alike. Scientists, military officials, and world leaders quickly realized that the situation was more than just an environmental anomaly—it was a crisis that defied logic and the natural order of the world.

In response, the **Global Research Initiative on Anomalous Phenomena (GRIAP)** was established. A team of experts from various fields—botany, physics, climatology, and environmental science—came together under the mandate of finding answers and solutions to the rapidly escalating tree crisis. This group of scientists, drawn from different nations, shared one urgent goal: to study the trees, understand their effects, and perhaps discover a way to stop them.

The Formation of GRIAP

Dr. Isabel Martinez, a highly respected botanist from Brazil, was among the first to be recruited to the group. Known for her groundbreaking work on plant biology and rapid growth patterns in tropical ecosystems, she was quickly appointed as one of the project's leads. But this was no ordinary research project—it was a race against time. Already, cities like São Paulo, New York, and Tokyo had been devastated by the emergence of the trees, and there was no telling where the next one would appear.

Martinez stood in the sterile, brightly lit conference room of the newly constructed GRIAP headquarters. Located in an undisclosed underground facility, far from the closest tree sites, the lab had been designed as a safe zone where the team could analyze samples and data without the constant threat of aberrations or the warping of reality that had been reported near the trees.

Around her, scientists buzzed with activity, coordinating field expeditions, poring over maps of affected areas, and running simulations. The air was tense—everyone knew the gravity of what they were facing. But there was also excitement, a shared belief that they were at the forefront of solving one of the greatest mysteries in human history.

Dr. David Johansson, a Swedish physicist, joined Martinez as co-lead. His expertise in spacetime anomalies had made him an invaluable asset in understanding the trees' effect on the fabric of reality. Johansson, usually calm and collected, looked unusually frazzled as he adjusted his glasses and flipped through satellite images of the trees' rapid growth.

"These things aren't just growing, Isabel," Johansson said quietly as they stood over one of the maps. "They're… breaking the rules. Look at these reports. Gravity anomalies, time dilation… We're not dealing with just a biological threat. The laws of physics don't apply the same way near these trees."

Martinez nodded, her mind racing. She had seen the early reports from Brazil before joining GRIAP, had witnessed firsthand the rapid mutation of plant life near the tree sites. Trees and plants that had once grown at natural rates were now growing ten times faster, exhibiting colors and behaviors that defied classification. But Johansson's words added a new layer of complexity to their work. They weren't just studying a biological threat—they were studying something far more profound.

Field Data Collection

The first few months of GRIAP's operation were spent gathering as much data as possible. Field teams were sent to tree sites all over the world, equipped with state-of-the-art technology to measure everything from soil composition to electromagnetic readings. But getting close to the trees was a dangerous task. The phenomena around the trees grew worse the closer one got—electronics malfunctioned, communication devices went dead, and some teams reported strange, unsettling sensations as if the very air was warping around them.

Martinez and Johansson reviewed one of the first major reports from a field team that had returned from a tree site in Argentina. The footage from the drone-mounted cameras showed the tree rising from the earth, its twisted branches stretching toward the sky. But it wasn't just the tree that was unusual. The plants surrounding it—once ordinary shrubs and bushes—had begun to change. Some glowed with a faint, otherworldly light. Others had grown thorns as long as a human arm, and their leaves shifted colors like a chameleon's skin. It was as if the tree's presence was mutating everything around it, transforming the environment into something unrecognizable.

Dr. Hannah Brody, the lead biologist on the Argentina expedition, stood in the briefing room, pale-faced as she gave her report. "The plant life in the immediate vicinity of the tree shows signs of accelerated growth—beyond anything we've seen in the natural world. But it's not just the growth rates. These plants are... hostile. The thorns orient themselves toward movement, almost like they're **aware**. We lost a drone to one of the larger vines. It pulled the drone out of the air and crushed it."

Martinez listened closely, her mind buzzing with questions. The trees weren't just altering the landscape—they were creating an environment that was actively hostile to any intrusion. The roots themselves seemed to dig deeper than anyone had anticipated, penetrating layers of bedrock and spreading far beyond the visible areas of the tree. The researchers couldn't explain how such massive growth was possible in such a short time, but the evidence was clear: these trees were rewriting the rules of biology, physics, and perhaps even reality.

Strange Anomalies and Early Discoveries

It wasn't long before GRIAP started receiving reports that couldn't be explained by any natural phenomenon. One of the most startling was the **time dilation effect**—researchers in close proximity to the trees reported that time seemed to pass differently around them. A team sent to monitor a tree in northern Canada had been gone for what felt like only a few hours, but when they returned, nearly an entire day had passed outside the zone of the tree's influence.

"This isn't just an atmospheric anomaly," Johansson explained during one of the debriefings. "Whatever the tree is emitting—whether it's energy, radiation, or something we don't even have a word for yet—it's distorting time and space. The closer we get, the worse it gets."

The time dilation, combined with the warping of gravity and the mutation of plant life, pointed to something far beyond what any of them had expected. The trees weren't just growing—they were altering the very fabric of the world around them.

Despite these early breakthroughs, progress was slow. Every time GRIAP sent teams to collect samples or data, something went wrong. Electronics failed, vehicles malfunctioned, and drones often returned with corrupted footage or none at all. Worse still, some of the researchers began to report strange hallucinations and nightmares after spending too much time near the trees. Dr. Brody had mentioned hearing voices—soft, barely perceptible whispers that seemed to come from the trees themselves.

Martinez dismissed it as stress, but deep down, she couldn't shake the feeling that something far more sinister was at play. The trees were **alive** in a way they didn't fully understand, and their presence was doing more than just reshaping the landscape—it was reshaping the people who came into contact with them.

The Inquisition's Watchful Eye

As GRIAP continued their research, another, more secretive organization began to take an interest in their work. The **Inquisition**, an ancient order rumored to be older than most governments, had long operated in the shadows, investigating anomalies that defied human understanding. Unlike the scientific community, the Inquisition had experience with phenomena that bridged the gap between science and something else—something far darker.

The Inquisition had been monitoring global anomalies for years, and the emergence of the trees caught their attention early on. Though they operated outside of official channels, they were well-connected, with agents embedded in military, government, and research organizations across the world. Two of their agents—Dr. Anton Koval and Dr. Sian Keller—had already infiltrated GRIAP, quietly gathering information and reporting back to their superiors.

To most of the GRIAP team, Koval and Keller were just highly skilled scientists. Koval, a geophysicist, had been instrumental in understanding the seismic activity near the trees, while Keller's background in epidemiology allowed her to track the strange biological changes in the environment. But while they contributed to the research, they were also steering it in subtle ways, ensuring that GRIAP's findings aligned with the Inquisition's goals.

The Inquisition wasn't interested in understanding the trees in the same way that Martinez and her team were. They weren't looking for scientific answers—they were looking for a way to control the situation, to harness the power of the trees for their own purposes. And if that meant keeping certain findings from reaching the public, so be it.

Koval, ever the pragmatist, quietly altered field reports, downplaying the more alarming anomalies and emphasizing the need for containment over investigation. Keller, meanwhile, kept a close eye on the other researchers, ensuring that no one got too close to the truth.

As the weeks passed, the Inquisition's influence grew, though few in GRIAP were aware of it. For now, their presence was subtle, a shadow hanging over the team's work. But as the trees continued to spread, warping the world around them, the Inquisition's true intentions would soon come to light.

CHAPTER 7
The Vagabond's Diary Begins

Isaac sat at his kitchen table, staring out the window at the twisted, nightmarish landscape that had once been his yard. The tree, now towering over his home, seemed to pulse with an unnatural life. Its branches curled and twisted in the windless sky, casting eerie, shifting shadows across the ground. The air around it shimmered with a sickly, iridescent glow, and the low hum that had haunted him for days persisted, vibrating in his bones.

He hadn't left the house in days, ever since the first creature—a grotesque mass of eyes and tendrils—had crawled free from one of the tree's strange cocoons. The memory of its many blinking eyes still haunted him, a constant reminder that reality itself had begun to unravel. And the world beyond his yard wasn't much better. The news reports were growing more chaotic, filled with images of similar trees erupting across the globe. Cities were falling, people were vanishing, and strange, twisted creatures were beginning to roam freely.

Isaac had been trying to make sense of it all, hoping for some kind of explanation, some way to stop the madness. But it all felt so far beyond his control, as though he were just a small, insignificant piece in some vast and terrible puzzle. His isolation weighed heavily on him, pressing down with the same suffocating tension that seemed to permeate the very air outside. His world had become smaller, reduced to the few rooms of his house and the looming tree outside. He could no longer trust his senses—the sounds and sights around him shifting in ways that made no sense.

That morning, as he tried to distract himself from the nightmarish view, Isaac began rummaging through the drawers of his kitchen, hoping to find something useful—perhaps a map or a radio, anything that could help him feel less disconnected from the world. As he searched, he found a small, battered book tucked in the back of one of the cabinets. At first, he thought it was one of his old journals, but as he pulled it out and flipped it open, he realized it wasn't his writing at all.

The cover was worn and cracked, the pages yellowed with age, but there was something about it that felt important, like it didn't belong there. He turned the first few pages, his eyes scanning the handwritten notes scrawled inside. The ink was faded, and the writing was rough, almost hurried, as if the author had been writing in a state of desperation.

Isaac's heart skipped a beat as he realized what he was holding: it was a diary. The pages were filled with entries, documenting someone else's experiences. Someone who had been traveling through areas affected by the tree.

The First Diary Entry

The first entry was dated only a few months earlier, around the time when Isaac had first noticed strange changes in his yard. The writer—who only referred to themselves as "the Vagabond"—described traveling through small towns that had begun to change in subtle, unsettling ways.

The Vagabond wrote:

"I don't know when it started, but I know now that there's no going back. The trees are growing everywhere. They burst from the ground like wounds in the earth, and nothing is the same anymore. The sky is wrong. The air is wrong. And the people... they're changing too."

Isaac felt a chill run down his spine as he read on, the words taking on a haunting familiarity. The Vagabond described towns where people had vanished without a trace, leaving behind empty streets and homes. In other places, the inhabitants hadn't vanished but had transformed—mutating in ways that defied explanation. They became twisted versions of themselves, their bodies contorted and stretched, their eyes filled with a hollow, unnatural light.

"They don't see it happening," the Vagabond wrote. "Or maybe they do, but they can't stop it. It's like they're trapped in their own nightmares, and the trees... the trees are feeding on them."

Isaac's hands trembled as he flipped through more of the entries. The Vagabond had traveled across several regions, documenting the changes they had witnessed. In one town, they described the plants beginning to glow, just like the ones Isaac had seen in his own yard. The trees there grew at impossible speeds, their branches reaching out as though they were alive, consuming everything in their path. People tried to escape, but the landscape warped and twisted around them, trapping them in place.

"I saw a man try to run," the Vagabond wrote. "He thought he could make it to the highway, but the road stretched and twisted like a snake. He ran for hours, but he never got any closer. The trees kept growing, and he kept running, until he finally disappeared. I don't know where he went. Maybe the trees swallowed him."

Isaac swallowed hard, his throat dry. The Vagabond's words mirrored his own experience—how he had tried to leave, only to find the world outside his yard shifting, making it impossible to escape. He had thought he was alone in this nightmare, but now, reading the diary, he realized that others had faced the same horrors. The trees were spreading everywhere, warping reality itself, trapping people in a twisted, ever-changing landscape.

The entry continued:

"I can't tell what's real anymore. Every time I close my eyes, I see the trees. They're in my dreams now, too. Their branches reach for me, their roots dig into

the ground beneath my feet. I try to run, but I can't move. The air is thick, like I'm breathing through mud. And the eyes... there are always eyes watching me."

Isaac shuddered. The creature he had seen in his yard—the one with all the eyes—flashed in his mind, and the memory sent a wave of nausea through him. Was this what was happening to him? Was he slowly being consumed by the tree's influence, just like the people in the Vagabond's diary?

Clues and Warnings

As Isaac continued reading, he realized that the Vagabond wasn't just documenting the horrors they had seen—they were trying to figure out how the trees worked. Each entry was filled with observations, notes on the trees' growth patterns, and theories about how the trees seemed to be connected to the land, the sky, and even the people near them.

"The trees don't just grow," the Vagabond wrote. *"They change everything around them. The plants, the animals, the people. It's like they're spreading a disease, infecting the land itself. And once the land is infected, there's no going back."*

The Vagabond had noticed the same strange phenomena that Isaac had experienced—how reality seemed to bend around the trees, how time felt different, how the very laws of nature seemed to break down in their presence. But there was something else, something deeper that the Vagabond hinted at but couldn't fully explain.

"I think the trees are alive," they wrote in one entry. *"Not just alive like plants. They're... sentient. They know we're here. They're watching us, learning from us. And they're feeding off of us. Every nightmare, every fear, every death—it makes them stronger."*

Isaac's breath caught in his throat. The idea was too terrifying to fully comprehend, but it made sense. The tree in his yard, the creatures that had emerged from its cocoons—it all felt deliberate, like something far beyond his understanding was pulling the strings, manipulating reality for some darker purpose.

"I don't know how much longer I can keep going," the Vagabond wrote in a later entry. *"Every town I pass through is worse than the last. People are either gone or... changed. The land itself is turning against us. I saw a man get strangled by vines today—vines that weren't there a moment before. It's like the trees are playing with us, letting us think we can escape, only to pull us back in."*

Isaac shut the diary for a moment, his hands shaking. He could barely process what he was reading. The Vagabond's experiences echoed his own fears, his own growing sense of dread. But there was something else, too—an urgency in the Vagabond's writing, a need to find answers. The diary wasn't just a record of the horrors the Vagabond had witnessed—it was a desperate attempt to understand what was happening, to find some way to survive.

But had the Vagabond succeeded? Had they found a way to escape the tree's influence, or had they, too, been consumed by the nightmare?

Isaac flipped to the last entry. The handwriting was shakier, more frantic than before.

"I think I'm close to something. I found a place where the trees haven't spread yet. It's far, deep in the mountains. I'm going there tomorrow. If I can just get away from the trees for a little while, maybe I'll find the answers I need. Maybe I'll find a way to stop them."

Isaac's heart raced. Could this place still exist? A place where the trees hadn't spread, where reality still held firm? The Vagabond had believed they were close to something, some kind of breakthrough.

But the final lines of the entry sent a chill down Isaac's spine.

THE SEED OF NIGHTMARES | 37

"I just hope it's not too late. I can feel them watching me now. The trees are everywhere. Even when I close my eyes, they're there. I don't know if I'll make it. But I have to try."

Isaac closed the diary and set it down on the table, his mind spinning. The Vagabond's words lingered in his thoughts, a haunting reminder that the nightmare was far from over. He didn't know if the Vagabond had survived, but their journey had revealed something crucial: the trees weren't just growing—they were evolving. And their influence was spreading faster than anyone had realized.

He stared out the window at the tree in his yard, its dark branches twisting against the blood-red sky. The hum in the air had grown louder, vibrating through his chest. The world outside was changing, mutating, and Isaac knew that he couldn't stay here much longer.

The Vagabond had seen the truth, and now Isaac was seeing it too. The trees weren't just a force of nature—they were something far more terrifying.

And they were watching.

CHAPTER 8
First Signs of Global Madness

Isaac awoke with a start, his heart pounding in his chest. He hadn't intended to fall asleep. In fact, sleep had become a rare and dangerous thing ever since the tree took root in his yard. The nightmares were relentless, twisted dreams where the branches of the tree reached for him, wrapped around him, pulling him into the ground. But something was different this time. His nightmare had felt more real, more tangible. The air had been thick with the smell of decay, and the weight of it still clung to him as he sat up, rubbing his eyes.

The house felt too quiet. Outside, the deep hum that had been vibrating through the earth since the tree's appearance had grown louder, more insistent. It was no longer a distant vibration but something that resonated in his bones, rattling his thoughts. He walked to the window, dreading what he would see but unable to stop himself.

The tree, its gnarled branches twisting in grotesque shapes, dominated his yard. But now, the sky had taken on a deeper, more menacing red, casting a sickly glow over everything. Isaac squinted, his breath catching as he noticed new shapes moving among the roots and shadows—more aberrations. Not just one or two like before, but a swarm of them, writhing and slithering through the twisted landscape. Each one was more grotesque than the last, some covered in eyes, others sporting limbs that bent at impossible angles. They moved with a disturbing fluidity, as if the warped reality around them had made their bodies malleable, capable of shifting in ways that defied the laws of nature.

The sight sent a cold shiver down his spine. The aberrations had become more frequent, more aggressive. Their numbers were increasing, and they no longer stayed near the tree. Isaac watched as they spread further, their dark forms creeping toward the street, toward the remnants of the world beyond his yard.

He felt a rising sense of dread as he realized that the tree's influence wasn't just confined to his home. The diary had warned him that the tree's corruption was spreading, and now it was clear. The once-familiar world outside was falling apart, and there was nothing he could do to stop it. He was trapped.

Isaac turned on the TV, desperate for any news, any shred of information that could make sense of what was happening. The news channels were chaotic, filled with fragmented reports and panicked journalists trying to piece together the global disaster. Every few minutes, the screen would flicker, the signal disrupted by strange electromagnetic interference.

He cycled through the channels, his pulse quickening as each report painted the same picture: the trees were spreading. Cities across the globe were in turmoil, each one reporting the same unnatural phenomena—impossible growths, creatures crawling from the ground, and the very fabric of reality breaking down around the trees.

A live feed from London showed people fleeing through the streets as massive roots tore up the pavement, twisting through buildings like serpents. The camera panned to the sky, showing a dark red moon hanging overhead, just like the one in Isaac's yard. The voice of the reporter was barely audible over the sound of screaming and the roar of collapsing buildings.

In New Delhi, a massive tree had burst from the center of a busy marketplace, its roots spreading out like veins through the city. People there were reporting time distortions—moments where hours passed in the blink of an eye or where entire days seemed to stretch endlessly. Scientists on the ground were at a loss to explain the phenomenon, but the fear was palpable. The footage showed people moving through the streets in a daze, confused and terrified as they tried to make sense of the warped time around them.

In Tokyo, entire neighborhoods had vanished, swallowed by the trees' roots. The broadcast showed footage of an eerily empty street, where the only sound was the distant hum of the tree. The buildings that remained seemed to flicker, as if they were caught between two realities, existing in both but belonging to neither.

Isaac flipped to another channel, showing a group of survivors gathered in a makeshift camp just outside Los Angeles. The camp had been hastily put together by the military, but even they seemed powerless to stop the spread of the trees. One survivor, his face pale with fear, described how the tree had appeared overnight, its roots tearing through his neighborhood in minutes. He had watched in horror as his neighbors had been trapped inside their homes, unable to escape as the ground swallowed them whole.

The survivor looked directly into the camera, his voice trembling. "It's like the world is folding in on itself. The trees—they're not just growing. They're… changing everything. Time doesn't feel right anymore. Gravity doesn't feel right. I can't explain it. You have to see it to believe it."

Isaac switched off the TV, feeling a sickening pit form in his stomach. The world was unraveling, and there was no denying it. The tree's influence was global, and the collapse of society had already begun.

The Research Group's Struggle

Despite the chaos, there were still those trying to understand the phenomenon. Among the most determined was the **Global Research Initiative on Anomalous Phenomena (GRIAP)**, the group of scientists Isaac had learned about from earlier news reports. Led by Dr. Isabel Martinez, the team had been working around the clock to gather data and analyze the trees, hoping to uncover a way to stop them. But their efforts were hampered at every turn—constant attacks on their labs, equipment failures, and the strange gravitational anomalies near the trees making data collection nearly impossible.

Dr. Martinez and her team had set up a research station on the outskirts of São Paulo, where one of the largest trees had erupted. The footage from their base, broadcast on one of the few remaining news channels, showed the team working in shifts, trying to map out the tree's growth patterns and its effects on the surrounding environment.

In a live briefing, Dr. Martinez appeared on screen, her face drawn with exhaustion but her voice steady. "We've been able to gather some preliminary data," she said, pointing to a series of charts on the screen behind her. "The trees are not only affecting plant life—they're altering the very fabric of reality. We're seeing gravity fluctuations and time distortions around the trees, with the effects worsening the closer you get. Some of our equipment is failing because the electromagnetic interference is off the charts. It's like nothing we've ever seen before."

Dr. David Johansson, a physicist on her team, stepped in, his expression grim. "What we're dealing with here isn't just a biological phenomenon. It's something far more profound. The trees are distorting space-time itself. In areas closest to the trees, time is no longer linear. Gravity isn't constant. We've observed objects floating, then crashing back to the ground. The implications of this are... staggering."

But even as they presented their findings, it was clear that the research team was running out of time. Reports from other labs indicated that the aberrations—those grotesque creatures born from the trees—were attacking research stations across the world. In some cases, entire facilities had been overrun, with no survivors.

Isaac watched as the footage cut to a scene outside one of the labs in Argentina. Aberrations—large, slithering masses of eyes and limbs—crawled across the landscape, smashing through the protective barriers and destroying equipment. The few scientists who remained fought to hold them back, but their weapons were ineffective. The aberrations moved through the wreckage, indifferent to the gunfire and explosions.

Dr. Martinez's voice came back on the screen. "We're losing labs faster than we can set them up. Our equipment is failing, our data is incomplete, and every attempt to get closer to the trees results in more casualties. But we can't stop. We have to keep trying. We need to understand what these trees are and what they want. Before it's too late."

The screen flickered, the transmission cutting in and out. Isaac could see the tension in Dr. Martinez's eyes—she was holding it together, but just barely. The weight of the world was on her shoulders, and the burden was growing heavier with each passing day.

Reality Begins to Unravel

Isaac turned away from the TV, his mind buzzing with the weight of the information. Gravity and time breaking down around the trees. Aberrations multiplying and attacking at will. The world's best scientists struggling to keep their labs intact while the very ground beneath them shifted and warped.

As the afternoon turned into evening, Isaac stepped outside, needing air, though the outside world offered little comfort. The tree in his yard had grown even larger, its branches curling upward like claws reaching for the blood-red sky. The hum was louder now, vibrating through the earth, making it hard to stand still. He felt off-balance, as if gravity itself was pulling him in strange directions.

Isaac walked to the edge of his yard, his eyes scanning the twisted landscape. The air seemed heavier, the ground beneath him feeling soft, almost fluid. He looked toward the horizon and saw the familiar shapes of the aberrations moving through the trees and streets, their distorted bodies blending with the unnatural shadows.

And then he noticed something else—a ripple in the air, like heat rising off asphalt. But this wasn't heat. It was... something else. Something he couldn't explain. The trees, the sky, the world around him—it all seemed to shimmer and warp, like a reflection in a pool of water that had been disturbed.

Time felt wrong. The seconds stretched and snapped back, moments slipping through his fingers. He blinked, trying to clear his mind, but the sensation only grew worse. The tree was bending reality around it, and Isaac could feel it pulling him in.

His stomach lurched as the ground seemed to tilt beneath him. He stumbled back, retreating toward the safety of his house. He couldn't stay outside anymore. The tree's influence was growing stronger, more aggressive, and Isaac knew that if he stayed out there too long, he might lose himself completely—lost in a place where time and space no longer followed any rules he understood.

Inside the house, Isaac sank into a chair, his hands shaking. The world outside was falling apart, and the nightmare was spreading faster than anyone could have predicted. The research team was fighting to understand it, but their resources were dwindling. The aberrations were growing in number, and reality itself was unraveling.

Isaac didn't know how much longer he could hold on.

The Underground Resistance Forms

Isaac sat in the dim glow of his living room, the air heavy with the relentless hum of the tree outside his window. Weeks of isolation had left him hollow, exhausted, and uncertain if he was slipping deeper into madness or if he was holding onto sanity by the thinnest of threads. The world outside was becoming unrecognizable, reality warping and twisting as the tree's influence spread further. His only lifeline to the outside world was the radio, an old analog model he had found buried in his basement, still working despite everything else falling apart.

He kept it tuned to different frequencies, hoping to catch snippets of information, the occasional desperate plea for help, or a fragment of a news broadcast that might tell him what was happening beyond his small, isolated world. But for days, there had been nothing but static—an endless, empty buzz that matched the oppressive hum of the tree.

But today, the static suddenly broke. A sharp crackle filled the room, and a voice, firm and steady, cut through the noise.

"This is the Underground Resistance. If anyone can hear this, we are fighting back. There is a safe haven 10 miles south of the old industrial park. If you're listening, you're not alone."

Isaac froze, his eyes widening. He hadn't heard a human voice in days. He leaned forward, heart pounding, as the broadcast continued.

"We know what you're facing. We know the trees are spreading, and the aberrations are getting stronger. We're holding our ground, but we need help.

If you're out there, you have to make it to the safe haven. You don't have to fight this alone."

Isaac's breath hitched in his throat. He stared at the radio, the voice crackling with static, the words both a promise and a challenge. It was the first time he had heard anyone speak with such certainty since the world had begun to fall apart. He reached out, his fingers trembling, and grabbed the radio's microphone. He hesitated, his mind racing. What if it was a trap? What if the Resistance was already gone, or worse—corrupted by the trees?

But the desperation to connect, to find some sense of hope, was overwhelming. He pressed the transmit button.

"I... I'm here," he said, his voice rough and unsteady. "Can you hear me? Are you there?"

For a moment, there was silence. His heart pounded in his chest, and he wondered if he had only imagined the voice. But then, the static wavered, and the voice returned, more urgent this time.

"Who is this? Are you safe?"

Isaac swallowed hard, feeling a surge of relief and fear all at once. "My name's Isaac. I'm— I'm near one of the large trees. I've been here for weeks. I can't... I can't get out."

The voice on the other end paused, as if considering. "Listen carefully, Isaac. You need to get out of there. The longer you stay near the tree, the more dangerous it becomes. Can you make it to the safe haven?"

Isaac looked out of the window at the massive, twisted branches of the tree dominating his yard. He had tried to leave before, but the landscape had shifted, the streets turning into an impossible labyrinth. The tree's influence had made it almost impossible to navigate.

"I don't know if I can," he admitted, his voice shaking. "Everything keeps changing. I don't know what's real anymore."

The voice softened, but the urgency remained. "We'll send someone to guide you. But you have to start moving now. We don't have much time. The aberrations are growing more aggressive, and the tree's influence will only get stronger. You have to trust us."

Isaac closed his eyes, feeling the weight of his fear pressing down on him. He knew staying here was a death sentence. He had seen what the tree could do—the nightmares, the hallucinations, the shifting shadows that seemed to crawl along the walls of his house. But leaving meant facing the unknown, stepping out into a world he no longer understood.

"I'll go," he said finally, forcing the words out. "I'll head south."

"Good," the voice said. "Stay off the main roads. Stick to the alleyways and side streets. We'll send someone to meet you halfway. Keep the radio on, and stay in contact. And Isaac... don't look back."

The transmission cut off abruptly, leaving Isaac alone in the silence once more. He stared at the radio, feeling a strange mix of fear and hope. For the first time in weeks, there was a direction—a goal, however tenuous. The Resistance was real, and they were fighting back. He wasn't alone.

A World Unraveling

Isaac grabbed his backpack and began to pack hastily. Supplies, a flashlight, extra batteries, the Vagabond's Diary—all the essentials he could carry. He had learned to move quickly, to be ready to leave at a moment's notice. The tree's influence was unpredictable, and he knew he had to make the most of every opportunity to escape.

He pulled on his jacket and took one last look around the house that had been his refuge for so long. It felt empty now, hollowed out by the presence of the tree that loomed just outside. He knew that staying meant succumbing to its power, to the madness it brought. He had to leave.

Isaac slipped out the back door, moving as quietly as he could. The air was heavy, the sky a dark shade of red that seemed to pulse with an unnatural energy. The streets were empty, the silence broken only by the distant howls of aberrations prowling the city's edges.

His heart pounded as he moved from shadow to shadow, following the directions the Resistance had given him. Every step felt like a gamble, the air thick with the presence of the tree's influence. The ground seemed to shift beneath his feet, the roads twisting in ways that made no sense. He glanced over his shoulder, half-expecting to see the tree following him, its branches reaching out like claws.

But he pressed on, clinging to the instructions the voice on the radio had given him. South. Ten miles south. The promise of a safe haven was all that kept him moving, even as his mind fought to make sense of the world around him.

The Resistance's Warning

After what felt like an eternity of navigating the distorted streets, the radio crackled to life again, the voice firm but hurried. "Isaac, are you there?"

"I'm here," Isaac whispered, trying to keep his voice steady.

"Good. Keep moving. We've got eyes on you, but you're not safe yet. The aberrations are drawn to movement near the trees, and they'll be on you if you slow down."

Isaac felt a cold sweat break out on his forehead. He quickened his pace, moving through narrow alleyways and over crumbling fences. The world seemed to shift and sway around him, the tree's presence pressing in from every direction.

He turned a corner and froze. In front of him, half-hidden in the shadows, was a figure—a man dressed in ragged clothes, his eyes wide with fear. For a moment, Isaac thought it was a hallucination, another trick of the tree. But then the man moved, waving him over.

"You must be Isaac," the man said, his voice low and urgent. "I'm Damon. We don't have much time. The safe haven's not far, but the path's dangerous. Follow me."

Isaac hesitated, his instincts screaming at him to run. But the desperation in Damon's eyes matched his own, and he knew he had no choice.

"Let's go," Isaac said, his voice steadier than he felt.

Damon led him through the twisted streets, navigating the shifting landscape with a confidence that surprised Isaac. It was clear that he knew these streets well, and Isaac wondered how long the Resistance had been operating in the shadows, fighting a battle that seemed increasingly impossible to win.

As they moved, Damon kept glancing back, his expression growing more tense with each passing moment. The air felt heavy, oppressive, and Isaac could feel the tree's influence pressing in from every direction.

"We're close," Damon said, his voice barely a whisper. "Just a little further."

They rounded a corner and froze. In the distance, the faint glow of a fire flickered, and Isaac could see movement—figures, indistinct and shadowy, shifting in the darkness.

"The aberrations," Damon hissed, pulling Isaac back into the shadows. "We need to move. Now."

They sprinted through the alley, their footsteps echoing off the cracked pavement. Isaac's heart pounded in his chest, his lungs burning with the effort, but he pushed on, driven by the promise of safety. The radio crackled in his pocket, a constant reminder that he wasn't alone—that there were others out there, fighting back.

For the first time in weeks, Isaac felt a spark of hope. It was fragile, fleeting, but it was enough to keep him going. The Resistance was real, and they had found him. Now, he just had to survive long enough to reach them.

CHAPTER 10

Second Diary Entry

Isaac sat at his kitchen table, the flickering light of the dying sun casting long shadows through the blood-red sky. His house had become his fortress, a place where he could try to escape the madness outside, but it felt more like a prison with every passing day. The air was thick with tension, an almost suffocating heaviness that made even the simplest task feel exhausting. The hum from the tree outside was constant now, vibrating through the walls, the floor, and into his very bones. He hadn't slept properly in days.

It had been a week since Isaac first discovered the **Vagabond's Diary**, and the strange, chaotic entries had haunted him ever since. The words on those pages mirrored what he had seen, what he had felt. The Vagabond had described the same eerie transformations—the trees growing at unnatural speeds, the land mutating, the people changing. And yet, Isaac still couldn't shake the feeling that things were getting worse, not just for him, but for the entire world.

As he stared out the window, watching the aberrations creep ever closer to his home, Isaac knew he needed to go back to the diary. Somehow, it seemed to hold answers, even if they were buried beneath layers of fear and desperation. He couldn't explain it, but the Vagabond's words felt like a lifeline, a connection to someone else who had faced the same horrors.

He picked up the worn book, the leather cover soft and cracked in his hands. The first entry had given him a glimpse into the Vagabond's journey, but there was so much more to uncover. He turned the pages slowly, his eyes scanning the hastily written lines until he reached the second entry.

The handwriting was shakier here, the words more frantic.

Vagabond's Diary - Second Entry

"I don't know where I am anymore. The world around me is collapsing, folding in on itself like a nightmare that I can't wake up from. I found a town—at least, I think it's a town. The buildings are still standing, but the people... they're not right. Nothing is right anymore. Everything feels like it's slipping away, like the ground isn't solid beneath my feet."

"The tree in this town is massive. It's taken over everything. The roots have split the roads, shattered the buildings. The air is thick, heavy, like it's pressing down on me, suffocating me. I can't breathe here. Every step I take feels like it's dragging me deeper into something I don't understand."

"The people... God, the people. They're trapped. Trapped in their own minds, I think. I see them wandering the streets, but they're not really there. It's like they're stuck in a dream they can't wake up from, like they're sleepwalking through a nightmare. I tried talking to one of them—a woman, her face blank, her eyes wide and unblinking. She didn't respond to anything I said, didn't even seem to see me. She just kept walking, mumbling something under her breath. I leaned in close, and I heard her whispering: 'It's not real. It's not real. It's not real.'"

"But it is real. It's all real. And that's the worst part."

Isaac's fingers tightened around the edges of the diary as he read the words. The Vagabond had found a town that had been completely overtaken by the tree's influence. It wasn't just the land or the environment that had changed—it was the people. They had become trapped, locked inside their own minds, unable to distinguish between reality and the nightmarish hallucinations the tree was forcing upon them.

Isaac's heart raced as he realized how similar the Vagabond's description was to what he had been experiencing. The air had felt heavier for days now, and there had been moments—fleeting, but terrifying—where Isaac had doubted his own senses. The world outside his window no longer felt stable. The ground seemed to shift and ripple like water, and there were times when the shadows moved on their own, twisting into grotesque shapes that he was sure couldn't be real.

But what if they were?

The thought made his skin crawl. Was he, too, beginning to lose his grip on reality? Was the tree somehow warping his mind, pulling him into a nightmare he couldn't escape?

He turned back to the diary, desperate for answers.

"I don't know how long I've been in this town. Time doesn't seem to work here anymore. It feels like I've been walking for days, but when I look at my watch, only a few hours have passed. The sky never changes. It's always red, always dark. The sun doesn't rise here. There's no night, no day. Just... endless twilight."

"I tried to leave, but I couldn't. Every road I took just led me back to the center of town, back to the tree. I walked for hours, but I never got any further away. It's like the town is folding in on itself, trapping me in some kind of loop. I can't escape."

"I see more of them now—the people, wandering aimlessly. They don't sleep. They don't eat. They just... exist. And I think... I think they're trapped in their nightmares. I can see it in their eyes. They're reliving something, over and over, something terrible. I don't know what, but I can feel it when I get close to them. It's like the air is thick with fear, with despair. I tried to help one of them—a young man who was sitting on the sidewalk, his face in his hands. But when I *touched him, he screamed. He looked at me like I was a monster, like I wasn't real."*

"Am I real? I don't know anymore."

Isaac felt a cold sweat break out across his skin as he read the words. The Vagabond had encountered something far worse than just the physical transformation of the land. The people in that town had been consumed by their own minds, their nightmares becoming indistinguishable from reality. And now, Isaac feared the same was happening to him.

He had been alone for so long, with only the tree and the aberrations as his company. The nights had been filled with strange sounds—whispers on the wind, disembodied voices that seemed to call to him from the darkness. He had tried to ignore them, to tell himself that it was just his mind playing tricks on him. But now, after reading the diary, he wasn't so sure.

The Vagabond had described a town where people were trapped in their nightmares, unable to break free. Isaac had seen the same thing in the fleeting moments when he dared to look outside—the way the world seemed to shift, the way time felt distorted. There had been moments when he wasn't sure if what he was seeing was real or just another hallucination.

The weight of the tree's presence was suffocating. The more time he spent near it, the more he felt his own thoughts slipping away, like sand through his fingers. The tree wasn't just warping the world outside—it was invading his mind.

He returned to the diary, hoping to find some clue, some way to resist the influence of the tree. But what he read next made his blood run cold.

"I don't think I'll make it out of this town. I've tried every way I can think of, but there's no escape. The tree has rooted itself too deeply, and the land is... wrong. Everything is wrong. The people here—they're gone, in every way that matters.

Their bodies are still moving, but their minds... they're somewhere else. Somewhere dark. I think I'm starting to hear the same whispers they are."

"It's the tree. I know it is. It's in their heads, in their dreams. It's feeding on them, turning their nightmares into reality. And now... now I think it's doing the same to me. I see things that shouldn't be there. I hear voices when there's no one around. I close my eyes, and the tree is there, waiting for me. I think it's always been there, watching, waiting for the right moment to take me."

"I don't know how much longer I can hold on. But if you're reading this... if you find this... know that the tree is more than just a plant. It's alive, and it's hungry. It wants us. All of us. And it will take us if we let it."

Isaac closed the diary, his hands trembling. The Vagabond's words echoed his own growing fear—that the tree wasn't just changing the world physically, but mentally. It was warping reality, trapping people in their nightmares, feeding on their fear and despair.

He stood up, his legs shaky, and walked to the window. The tree outside his yard loomed larger than ever, its dark branches twisting and curling in the windless air. The hum was louder now, a deep, resonant vibration that filled his chest, his head, his thoughts.

Isaac pressed his hand against the glass, staring at the nightmare that had become his world. The Vagabond's words were clear: the tree was alive, and it was coming for him. It was only a matter of time before the line between reality and nightmare blurred completely.

And when that happened, there would be no escape.

CHAPTER 11
Early Research Discoveries

Dr. Isabel Martinez sat hunched over a table covered with maps, soil samples, and stacks of data printouts. The research station was a mess of activity, with team members rushing in and out of the main lab, their faces tight with the kind of stress only found in the midst of an unprecedented catastrophe. The low hum of generators filled the air, the only sound apart from the soft clinking of test tubes and the occasional murmurs of hurried conversation. The world outside was crumbling, and the clock was ticking for all of them.

She rubbed her temples, trying to stave off the headache that had been throbbing behind her eyes for the past few days. Sleep had become a luxury she could no longer afford. Since the tree had first appeared near São Paulo, it had been one long, frantic sprint to gather as much data as possible before things spiraled out of control.

And they were spiraling faster than she could keep up.

Her team had been among the first to observe the tree's growth pattern, and now, they were witnessing something far more disturbing than just rapid biological development. The tree wasn't just changing the environment—it was warping reality itself.

Dr. David Johansson, the team's physicist, stepped into the room, a grim expression etched on his face. He held a tablet in his hand, its screen flickering slightly from the persistent electromagnetic interference that had been plaguing their instruments since the tree first emerged.

"Isabel," he said, placing the tablet on the table in front of her. "You need to see this."

Martinez looked up, the fatigue evident in her eyes. "More anomalies?"

Johansson nodded. "Worse than before. Take a look at the readings from the last drone we sent into the proximity zone."

He tapped the screen, bringing up a series of charts and graphs. Martinez leaned in, scanning the data. Her heart sank. The readings were unlike anything she had ever seen. Gravitational fluctuations, time distortions, and a rapid increase in ambient electromagnetic energy. All of it centered around the tree's influence.

"What is this?" she asked, her voice low, almost disbelieving.

Johansson sighed and ran a hand through his hair. "We've been monitoring these anomalies for a while now, but they're getting more extreme. The closer we get to the tree, the less stable reality becomes. Gravity is fluctuating in ways we can't predict. Time seems to be... collapsing in on itself."

Martinez stared at the screen, her mind racing to process what she was seeing. Gravity and time—the very forces that held their world together—were being disrupted by the tree's presence. She had known from the beginning that this was no ordinary biological phenomenon, but this... this was something far beyond their understanding.

"I don't know how to explain it," Johansson continued. "It's like the tree is tapping into something deeper, something fundamental. It's not just growing—it's changing the rules of reality. I've never seen anything like it."

Martinez sat back in her chair, her eyes drifting to the window. Outside, the tree loomed over the horizon, its dark, twisted branches reaching toward the blood-red sky. The air around it seemed to shimmer, as though the very atmosphere was warping under its influence.

The team had already documented strange growths in the plant life surrounding the tree. Ordinary plants had mutated, growing at impossible speeds, their leaves glowing with an unnatural light. Some of the plants had even developed strange, hostile behaviors. One of their drones had been destroyed by a vine that had shot out from the ground, wrapping around the machine and crushing it before they could pull it back.

But it wasn't just the plants. The wildlife in the area had changed too. Animals that had once been harmless—rabbits, deer, even birds—had begun to mutate. They had grown larger, more aggressive, their bodies warping in ways that defied biology. Some of the team had reported seeing animals with extra limbs, glowing eyes, and other grotesque alterations.

One of the researchers had found a rabbit near the edge of the tree's influence, its body covered in strange, iridescent fur. The creature had been disoriented, twitching uncontrollably as if it couldn't understand the world around it. They had taken it back to the lab for study, but within hours, the rabbit had died, its body breaking down as if it had been unable to cope with the changes forced upon it.

Everything around the tree was mutating—changing into something unrecognizable. And it wasn't just the environment.

Martinez turned back to Johansson, her voice steady despite the rising fear in her chest. "And the people?"

Johansson hesitated. "It's getting worse. You know about the early cases—the hallucinations, the disorientation. But now it's escalating. Some of the field teams have reported severe psychological breakdowns. It's like their minds can't handle being near the tree for too long."

Martinez clenched her fists. This was the part that disturbed her the most. The physical changes in the environment were terrifying enough, but the way the tree seemed to be affecting people's minds—that was something she hadn't expected. They had lost three members of the team in the last week, each one succumbing to what was now being called **Tree Psychosis**.

It started with headaches and nightmares, visions of the tree's twisted branches and the grotesque creatures that crawled from its roots. But soon, it became something more—paranoia, confusion, a complete disconnection from reality. Those affected would wander aimlessly, muttering to themselves, unable to distinguish between what was real and what was a hallucination. And then, they would disappear—wandering into the forest of mutated trees, never to return.

Martinez had seen it happen firsthand. One of their researchers, Dr. Tessa Alvaro, had been working on analyzing soil samples when she started showing signs of the condition. At first, it was subtle—she had trouble focusing, kept mentioning strange dreams. But within days, her behavior had grown erratic. She claimed to hear voices coming from the tree, whispering her name, calling her closer. And then one morning, she was gone. They found her shoes and her field journal near the edge of the tree's influence, but there was no sign of her. Just an empty space where the forest had swallowed her up.

The team had tried to document the effects, but every time they sent people in to investigate, the symptoms started to appear. The closer they got to the tree, the stronger the influence. It wasn't long before they realized they couldn't send anyone in without risking losing more team members.

Johansson broke the silence. "I think the tree is feeding on them."

Martinez turned to him, her brow furrowing. "What do you mean?"

He gestured to the tablet. "These readings—the fluctuations, the anomalies—it's almost as if the tree is drawing power from the people around it. The longer they stay near the tree, the more it distorts their minds. It's like it's amplifying their fears, their nightmares, and using that to grow stronger. Every time we lose someone to Tree Psychosis, the tree gets bigger. The roots spread further. The environment changes faster."

Martinez felt a chill run down her spine. The idea that the tree was feeding off the very minds of the people near it was horrifying, but it made a terrible kind of sense. The tree wasn't just a physical threat—it was a psychological one as well. It was warping reality, not just for the land and the animals, but for the people too.

She stood up, pacing the room as she tried to process everything. "We need to warn the others," she said. "The public needs to know what's happening."

Johansson frowned. "Are you sure that's a good idea? If we release this information now, it could cause a panic. People are already terrified. If they learn that the trees are affecting their minds—"

"They deserve to know," Martinez interrupted, her voice firm. "We can't keep this quiet. If people don't know what they're dealing with, they'll keep getting closer to the trees, thinking they can fight back. But they can't. Not if this... psychosis is part of the equation. We need to start developing countermeasures."

Johansson nodded, though his expression remained grim. "I agree. But how do we fight something that's warping the very fabric of reality?"

Martinez didn't have an answer. That was the question that had been haunting her ever since the trees had appeared. How did you fight something that didn't obey the laws of nature, something that could twist time, gravity, and even human minds to its will?

She glanced back at the tablet, her eyes scanning the disturbing data once more. The tree's influence was growing, spreading outwards with each passing day. And now, it wasn't just the land and the wildlife that were being affected—it was the people. Tree Psychosis was just the beginning, a warning of what was to come.

"We need to act fast," Martinez said quietly. "Before the tree takes everything."

CHAPTER 12
Resistance's First Major Strike

Isaac had spent the last several days locked in his home, his only connection to the world outside being the faint, garbled radio transmissions that still reached him. The world beyond his yard had descended into chaos. The news had all but stopped, leaving only static-filled broadcasts from scattered groups of survivors. But among these fragments of communication, there was one name that kept coming up more and more: **Kellar**.

The rumors about the Underground Resistance had spread quickly, despite the collapse of society. They were a group of fighters, outcasts, and survivors who had banded together to strike back against the aberrations and the growing influence of the trees. Isaac had heard whispers of their efforts—brief reports of small victories, moments of defiance in a world falling apart. But today, the radio crackled with something new. Something bigger.

"... Resistance hit the outskirts of Phoenix. Major strike on the aberrations... casualties reported, but they... managed to push them back. Kellar led the charge."

Isaac leaned closer to the radio, his heart pounding. He could hardly believe what he was hearing. The Resistance had launched a major assault? They had fought the aberrations head-on, and—somehow—survived?

"... lost nearly half their squad, but the aberrations retreated... civilians rescued... fighting's growing more intense..."

The transmission cut out again, leaving Isaac sitting in stunned silence. Half their squad, gone. But they had fought back. They had rescued people. It wasn't much, but in this new world, even the smallest victory felt monumental. For the first time in weeks, Isaac felt something that resembled hope—a flicker of it, fragile and small, but real.

But while Isaac's thoughts were filled with the Resistance's apparent success, the truth on the ground was far more brutal.

Kellar's First Major Strike

Kellar crouched behind the crumbling remnants of what had once been a freeway overpass, his breath coming in ragged bursts. His body ached, every muscle protesting against the grueling battle they had just fought, but there was no time to rest. The air around him was thick with the smell of burning metal and blood, a mixture of human and aberration alike.

The raid on Phoenix was supposed to be a turning point, a moment where the Resistance could show that the aberrations could be fought, could be defeated. Kellar had spent weeks planning it, gathering what little intel they had, and piecing together a strike team with the best scavenged tech they could find. It was supposed to be a strategic hit—a precision strike on one of the larger nests of aberrations that had taken root on the outskirts of the city.

But nothing had gone as planned.

The Resistance had set up their base in an old, abandoned warehouse several miles from the Phoenix city center. Kellar had chosen the location because of its isolation, its proximity to a supply of still-functioning tech, and the fact that the aberrations hadn't yet overrun the area. They had been monitoring the nest for days, trying to get a sense of how many creatures were inside, what kind of threat they were up against. The plan was simple: get in fast, hit them hard, and rescue any civilians they could find before pulling out.

Kellar's team was made up of about twenty fighters—ex-soldiers like him, as well as a few civilians who had shown they could handle themselves in a fight.

They were equipped with whatever weapons they had managed to scavenge: old rifles, makeshift explosives, and a few pieces of experimental tech they had managed to steal from a government research facility. The tech was unstable, but it was all they had.

As they approached the nest, hidden within the ruins of an old industrial district, the air had grown colder, heavier. Kellar had known immediately that they were close. The trees—always the trees—were there, looming in the distance, their roots twisting through the crumbling buildings like veins through a corpse. And with the trees came the aberrations.

The nest had been bigger than they expected. Aberrations of all shapes and sizes swarmed the area, their grotesque bodies writhing and twisting as they moved. Some were massive, lumbering beasts with thick, armored hides, while others were smaller, more agile, their many eyes glowing in the dim light. They moved with a disturbing grace, their bodies flowing through the ruined landscape like water.

Kellar had given the signal, and the Resistance had moved in, their weapons trained on the creatures. The first explosion had rocked the nest, tearing through the twisted metal and concrete of the old factories. Aberrations screeched as they were engulfed in flames, their bodies convulsing as the makeshift bombs ripped through them.

For a moment, it had seemed like they had the upper hand. The aberrations were caught off guard, their ranks thrown into disarray by the sudden assault. Kellar's team pressed forward, firing into the mass of creatures, picking off the smaller ones as they moved deeper into the nest.

But then, the aberrations adapted.

The larger creatures, seemingly impervious to the Resistance's weapons, began to charge. They moved with a terrifying speed, their massive limbs crushing anything in their path. One of the Resistance fighters—Lina, a woman who had survived the fall of San Francisco—was caught in the path of a charging aberration. Kellar had shouted for her to move, but it was too late. The creature barreled into her, its thick, spiked limbs piercing her body. She was dead before she hit the ground.

Kellar had barely had time to process her death before the rest of the aberrations descended on them. The battle became a desperate struggle for survival, the Resistance forced to fall back as the creatures swarmed around them. The scavenged tech they had brought with them—a crude EMP device meant to disable the aberrations' strange electromagnetic fields—had malfunctioned almost immediately, leaving them with nothing but their rifles and explosives.

They fought as best they could, but the casualties mounted quickly. One by one, Kellar's fighters fell—ripped apart by the aberrations' claws, crushed beneath their massive limbs, or worse, consumed by the strange, pulsating cocoons that had begun to appear around the trees.

By the time the aberrations had retreated, half of Kellar's team was dead. Finn, one of his closest allies, had been dragged into one of the cocoons before Kellar could reach him. The last thing Kellar had seen was Finn's face, twisted in agony as the cocoon enveloped him, pulling him into its dark, pulsating depths.

Kellar had pulled the survivors back to the remains of the overpass, his mind racing. The mission had been a disaster. They had destroyed a few aberrations, but at what cost? Half his team was gone, and the nest was still standing. The tech they had relied on had failed, and the aberrations were stronger than ever.

As he sat there, catching his breath, the bitterness began to creep in. They had been fools to think they could fight this. The aberrations weren't something you could just kill. They were part of something bigger, something that couldn't be stopped with bullets and bombs.

He had lost too many people—good people—and for what? A few dead creatures and a handful of rescued civilians?

Kellar's hands clenched into fists. He was angry. Angry at the aberrations. Angry at the trees. Angry at the world for falling apart so completely. But most of all, he was angry at himself for believing they could make a difference.

One of the survivors, a young man named Marcus, approached him, his face pale and drawn. "What do we do now, Kellar?"

Kellar looked up at him, his expression hard. "We keep fighting."

"Fighting for what?" Marcus asked, his voice cracking. "We lost half our team. We can't keep doing this."

Kellar stood, his body trembling with exhaustion and anger. "We don't have a choice," he said, his voice cold. "This is all we've got. We either fight, or we die. And I'm not going down without taking as many of those things with me as I can."

Marcus looked at him for a long moment, then nodded, though his face betrayed his doubt. The rest of the survivors gathered around Kellar, their expressions a mix of fear, exhaustion, and hopelessness.

Kellar knew their morale was shattered. He had pushed them too hard, taken them too far into a battle they couldn't win. But what else could they do? The aberrations were spreading, and the trees were growing stronger every day. If they didn't fight, the world would be consumed. But the losses were mounting, and Kellar could feel his grip on the group slipping.

He wasn't the leader they needed. Not anymore. He was too bitter, too reckless, too consumed by his own rage.

Isaac Hears the News

Back in his house, Isaac sat by the radio, listening to the fragmented reports of the Resistance's strike. They had lost many, but they had fought back.

Despite the heavy casualties, the idea that someone—anyone—was pushing against the tide of aberrations gave him a sliver of hope.

Isaac knew he couldn't join them. Not yet. The world outside his home was too warped, too dangerous. The tree in his yard was growing stronger by the day, and the aberrations were becoming bolder, venturing closer and closer to his front door. But knowing that there were people out there, people like Kellar, still fighting—it gave him a reason to hold on.

Maybe, just maybe, there was still a chance.

CHAPTER 13
Tensions in the Research Group

The dim lights of the underground research facility flickered as the steady hum of the generators provided a semblance of normalcy amidst the chaos outside. Deep beneath the surface, the team at the **Global Research Initiative on Anomalous Phenomena (GRIAP)** worked tirelessly, their focus on understanding the trees that were now warping reality and spreading across the globe. Dr. Isabel Martinez sat at the head of the long, cluttered table in the facility's main conference room, surrounded by her fellow scientists. Their faces were etched with fatigue, fear, and something else—doubt.

For months, they had been studying the trees, gathering as much data as they could from increasingly dangerous field missions. Every discovery seemed to raise more questions than answers. The electromagnetic disturbances, the gravitational anomalies, the mutations in plant and animal life, and most disturbingly, the impact the trees were having on human minds—**Tree Psychosis** was a reality they could no longer ignore.

But now, an entirely different debate was raging, one that had been simmering beneath the surface for weeks and was finally boiling over.

"We can't keep sitting on this information," Dr. Martinez said, her voice firm but exhausted. She looked around the table at her colleagues, each one of them weathered by months of stress and dwindling hope. "The public has a right to know what we've discovered. If people don't understand the full scope of what we're facing, they're going to keep walking into these tree zones thinking they can escape. We need to warn them."

Dr. David Johansson, sitting across from her, shook his head slowly. His glasses were perched on the edge of his nose, his face grim. "Isabel, I get where you're coming from. I do. But what good is releasing this information going to do? We've barely scratched the surface of understanding these trees. All we have are theories and partial data. If we go public with this now, all we're going to do is cause mass panic."

A murmur of agreement rippled through the room. Dr. Elaine Parson, the head of the facility's psychological studies unit, nodded in agreement with Johansson. "We've already seen what Tree Psychosis can do," she added, her voice calm but tense. "If people hear that the trees are distorting reality, warping their minds... they'll lose it. They'll go mad just thinking about it. Panic will spread faster than the trees themselves."

Martinez clenched her fists under the table. She knew the risks, but she also knew that keeping the world in the dark was not the answer. The team had seen firsthand the devastating effects of the trees. People were dying, cities were collapsing, and more and more aberrations were appearing with each passing day. The longer they waited to share their findings, the worse things would get.

"I'm not saying we have to release every detail," Martinez argued. "But people need to understand that the trees aren't just growing—they're changing everything around them. They're warping reality, and the longer people stay near them, the more their minds are at risk. We've seen what happens to people who spend too much time in these zones. They lose themselves. They become part of the trees' influence."

Johansson sighed, rubbing his temples. "We don't even fully understand the scope of the threat ourselves. What if we release this information and people start making bad decisions based on incomplete data? What if governments respond with force, only making things worse? We've already seen how ineffective conventional weapons are against the trees and the aberrations. The last thing we need is more chaos."

Martinez leaned forward, her eyes sharp. "We don't have time to wait for complete data. Every day, more people are dying. Every day, more trees are taking root. If we don't give people the information they need to protect themselves, they'll keep making the same mistakes. And Tree Psychosis is spreading faster than we anticipated. We've lost too many already."

Her voice caught for a moment, the memory of Dr. Tessa Alvaro—one of their brightest researchers—still fresh in her mind. Tessa had been consumed by Tree Psychosis after weeks of exposure to the trees. Martinez had watched helplessly as the once brilliant scientist descended into madness, mumbling incoherently about whispers from the trees before wandering into the woods, never to return.

At the far end of the table, Dr. Anton Koval cleared his throat. He had been silent for most of the discussion, but now his voice cut through the tension in the room like a knife.

"I agree with Dr. Martinez," Koval said, his voice low but steady. "People need to know what they're dealing with. We can't keep hiding behind incomplete data. The public deserves to know what's out there, what's happening to their world."

Martinez glanced at Koval, a flicker of gratitude in her eyes. She didn't know him well—he had only joined the team a few months ago—but he had proven to be a valuable asset. Koval was a geophysicist, and his insights into the seismic activity around the trees had been crucial in understanding how deep the roots of the phenomenon went, both literally and figuratively.

But there was something about him that unsettled her. He was always composed, too composed. His calmness in the face of the escalating crisis seemed unnatural, almost as if he knew more than he let on.

Dr. Sian Keller, sitting beside Koval, nodded in agreement. "It's time to stop playing it safe," she said. "We've been playing defense for too long. The world is falling apart, and the longer we wait, the harder it's going to be to stop it. People need to know what they're up against."

The room grew silent as the weight of the debate settled on everyone's shoulders. Martinez could feel the tension in the air. It wasn't just about the data anymore—it was about the responsibility they had as scientists, as people who had seen the truth behind the nightmare that was unfolding.

But there was something else at play, something deeper that Martinez couldn't quite put her finger on.

The Inquisition's Influence

Unbeknownst to most of the research team, Koval and Keller were not just scientists—they were agents of the **Inquisition**, a shadowy organization that had been monitoring global anomalies for centuries. The Inquisition had seen this kind of threat before, though not on this scale, and they had their own agenda. Their mission was to contain the trees, not necessarily to understand them. They didn't care about the public's right to know. In fact, they believed that the less the world knew, the better.

Koval and Keller had been quietly working to undermine the efforts of the research team for weeks. They had been steering the research in directions that suited the Inquisition's goals, subtly altering reports, downplaying the most alarming findings, and ensuring that key discoveries stayed out of the public eye. The Inquisition wanted control, and control required secrecy.

As the debate raged on, Koval and Keller exchanged a glance. They had already made their decision. The research group's internal conflicts were playing right into their hands.

Koval leaned forward, his expression unreadable. "I think we're missing the bigger picture here," he said, his voice calm. "It's not just about the trees—it's about maintaining order. If we release this information now, without a solid plan in place, we risk causing widespread panic. We've seen what happens when people panic. They make irrational decisions, and that could lead to even more loss of life."

Dr. Elaine Parson nodded, her face tight with worry. "He's right. Panic could lead to violence, to people lashing out in ways we can't control. We need to be careful."

Martinez stared at Koval, something about his words making her uneasy. He was speaking sense, but there was a coldness to his logic, a detachment that didn't sit right with her.

"We can't let fear paralyze us," she said, her voice firm. "Yes, people might panic, but they have a right to know the truth. If we keep this information to ourselves, we're no better than the governments that are trying to suppress the severity of this crisis. We're scientists. It's our job to provide the facts, not hide them."

Koval met her gaze, his expression unreadable. "I understand your passion, Isabel. But we have to think about the long-term consequences. We're dealing with forces beyond our comprehension. This isn't just about science anymore. It's about survival."

The room fell silent once again as the team considered Koval's words.

Martinez felt the weight of the decision pressing down on her. She knew she was right, but she also knew that fear and doubt were powerful forces, even among the most rational of minds. The team was fracturing, and she didn't know how much longer she could hold them together.

Finally, Dr. Johansson broke the silence. "We need more time," he said, his voice weary. "We need to gather more data before we make any rash decisions. Let's not rush into this."

Martinez opened her mouth to protest, but Koval cut her off. "Let's take a step back," he said smoothly. "We're all exhausted. We've been working nonstop for months. Let's revisit this discussion after we've had some time to rest and think things through."

Reluctantly, Martinez nodded, though the knot in her stomach told her that something wasn't right.

As the team began to disperse, Koval and Keller exchanged another glance. They had succeeded in delaying the release of the findings—for now. But the Inquisition's grip on the situation was tightening. And soon, they would have to make their move.

Martinez remained seated at the table, her thoughts swirling. She knew they were running out of time. The trees were spreading, the aberrations were growing stronger, and the world was falling apart.

She just didn't know how much longer they could afford to wait.

Chapter 14

Psychological Toll

Isaac sat in the corner of his living room, knees pulled to his chest, staring blankly at the twisted, pulsing shadows that danced across the walls. He hadn't slept in days—at least, he didn't think he had. Time had lost all meaning. The once familiar ticking of the clock had stopped making sense, the hands moving erratically, sometimes speeding up, other times slowing down until they seemed frozen in place.

The tree outside his house was growing stronger, more dominant, and with each passing hour, its influence crept deeper into his mind. The constant hum—low, pervasive, vibrating through the walls—never stopped. It was always there, pressing in on him, like some kind of malignant presence whispering in his ear. And the nightmares… they were getting worse.

Every time Isaac closed his eyes, he was there again, beneath the tree's gnarled branches. In his dreams, the sky was black, not red, and the roots of the tree stretched endlessly across the earth, wrapping around buildings, cities, and mountains, pulling them down into a void. He would run, always running, but no matter how far he went, the tree was there, waiting for him. Its branches reached out, its roots burrowed into his skin, pulling him down into the earth where there was nothing but darkness, the sound of his own heartbeat, and the endless, unrelenting hum.

And then, when he woke up, the line between reality and the nightmare blurred. The world around him twisted and shifted, shadows flickering at the edge of his vision, shapes moving where there should have been nothing. Sometimes, he would see faces—vague, indistinct faces in the walls, in the windows, in the branches of the tree. They never spoke, but their eyes followed him, watching, always watching.

Isaac didn't know how much longer he could take it.

Yet, in spite of the growing terror gnawing at his sanity, there was something else that kept him going. **Curiosity.** An obsessive need to understand what was happening. To find some kind of meaning in the chaos. Ever since he'd found the **Vagabond's Diary**, the strange, disconnected entries had haunted him. The Vagabond had described their descent into madness, the same madness Isaac now felt pulling at the edges of his mind. But somewhere within those frantic words had been hints—clues that suggested the tree's influence wasn't just some random, malevolent force. There was a purpose behind it.

The problem was, Isaac was losing his ability to trust his own senses. Was anything he was seeing or hearing real anymore? The tree's influence had invaded his thoughts, corrupted his perception of the world. He'd started questioning everything, wondering if the world outside his house still existed in the same form or if it had crumbled completely into nightmare. There was no way to tell.

His hands shook as he reached for the notebook where he had started keeping his own observations. It was a futile attempt to hold on to some sense of control, to create a narrative that might explain what was happening. He flipped through the pages, scanning the chaotic jumble of notes he had written over the past week.

The air is heavier near the tree. Harder to breathe. The hum is growing louder, but I can't tell if it's the tree or my own thoughts. There's something inside it. I can feel it watching.

The clock stopped yesterday. It's still moving, but the hands don't make sense. Sometimes, it feels like hours pass in a minute. Sometimes, time stretches so thin I can hear it cracking.

I saw someone outside yesterday. Or maybe it was a dream. I don't know anymore. They were walking, but they weren't walking right. Like they were stuck in place, their feet moving, but they weren't getting anywhere.

Everything is slipping. I'm slipping.

Isaac closed the notebook, his hands trembling. The more he tried to understand, the more his mind twisted itself in knots. Every question he asked only led to more questions, none of which had answers. But he couldn't stop. The tree was doing something to him, to the world, and he needed to know what.

The Research Group's Breakthrough

Meanwhile, hundreds of miles away, deep within the underground research facility, Dr. Isabel Martinez stared at the series of equations and simulations projected on the screen in front of her. Her eyes were bloodshot from lack of sleep, her mind racing as she and her team began to unravel the deeper implications of the tree's presence.

For weeks, they had been collecting data from the areas surrounding the trees—seismic activity, gravitational anomalies, electromagnetic disturbances. But now, something had clicked. The pieces of the puzzle were starting to fall into place, and it was more horrifying than any of them had anticipated.

Dr. David Johansson, the team's physicist, stood beside her, his hands gripping the edge of the table as he watched the data unfold. "It's not just warping space," he said quietly. "It's doing something to time as well."

Martinez nodded, her eyes scanning the simulation. The gravitational anomalies near the tree had been the first clue—places where gravity seemed to fluctuate unpredictably, pulling at objects and distorting their movement. But now, they were starting to see the same fluctuations in the flow of time itself.

Johansson pointed to a section of the data. "Look at this. This was taken near one of the largest trees in New Mexico. The gravitational pull is off the charts, but look at the temporal readings. Time is slowing down near the tree, almost as if it's being stretched."

Martinez leaned in, her mind racing. "How is that possible? Is the tree affecting the space-time continuum itself?"

"I don't know," Johansson admitted. "But we're seeing the same pattern in multiple locations. It's like the trees are bending the rules of reality, reshaping the fabric of existence. Gravity, time, even space itself—none of it behaves the way it's supposed to near these things."

Martinez rubbed her temples, trying to fight the growing headache. "And Tree Psychosis? Could this be part of it? If time and space are being distorted, could that be why people are losing their grip on reality?"

Johansson frowned. "It's possible. If time is warping, people's perception of it would be affected. They might experience hours as seconds, or seconds as hours. It could explain the disorientation, the hallucinations. But there's more to it than that. The trees are... influencing thoughts, pulling on something deeper."

Martinez felt a cold shiver run down her spine. She had suspected as much. The trees weren't just physical anomalies—they were reaching into people's minds, distorting their perception of reality. She thought of the people they had lost—researchers who had succumbed to Tree Psychosis, wandering into the woods, mumbling incoherent things about voices and shadows that weren't there.

Or maybe they were.

"We need more data," Martinez said, her voice strained. "We need to understand how the trees are doing this, what they're connected to. There's something deeper going on here, something beyond just biological mutation or gravitational disturbances. The trees are alive, and they're changing everything around them, including us."

Johansson nodded grimly. "Agreed. But we're running out of time. The trees are spreading faster than we can study them. If we don't figure this out soon, there won't be anything left to save."

Martinez sighed, feeling the weight of the world on her shoulders. They had come so far, uncovered so much, but the more they learned, the more impossible the task seemed. How could they stop something that defied the very laws of nature? Something that was bending time, warping space, and reaching into people's minds to pull them apart from the inside?

As the team continued their work, Martinez couldn't shake the feeling that they were missing something, some crucial piece of information that could make sense of the chaos. But for now, all they had were theories and incomplete data—and the terrifying realization that the trees were far more dangerous than they had ever imagined.

Isaac's Descent

Isaac stood at the window, staring at the tree as its branches twisted in the blood-red sky. He could feel it—deep in his bones, in his thoughts. The tree was pulling on him, dragging him into its influence. Time didn't make sense anymore. The days and nights blurred together, and sometimes, he wasn't even sure if he was awake or dreaming.

He thought about the **Vagabond's Diary**, about how the writer had described the same feelings—the same confusion, the same loss of reality. The tree had taken the Vagabond, and now it was coming for him.

But Isaac wasn't ready to give up. He wasn't ready to surrender to the madness. There had to be a way to understand what was happening, to find a way out of the nightmare. The tree was changing the rules of reality, but if he could figure out how, maybe he could fight back. Maybe he could escape.

His eyes flickered to the notebook on the table. The answers had to be there, somewhere in the chaos of his own thoughts. He just had to hold on long enough to find them.

But as the tree's influence grew stronger, and the line between dream and reality blurred further, Isaac knew he was running out of time.

CHAPTER 15
The Vagabond's Diary —Mutating Wildlife

The shadows in Isaac's home had grown longer, darker, and more twisted than ever. It was as if the very walls of his house had absorbed the madness seeping in from outside, warping them along with his thoughts. The air felt thick and oppressive, the hum of the tree outside his window vibrating constantly through his bones. Isaac hadn't dared venture beyond his front door for days, but the view from the window told him enough: the world was changing, mutating under the tree's influence.

He had spent the last few hours reading and rereading the **Vagabond's Diary**, trying to make sense of it all. The Vagabond's experiences seemed to mirror his own, yet they offered no comfort—only a grim realization that the horrors Isaac was living through were not unique to him. The trees were spreading everywhere, infecting everything.

Isaac opened the diary to the next entry. The third entry. His fingers shook slightly as he began to read, the familiar sense of dread creeping up on him like a slow-moving fog.

Vagabond's Diary – Third Entry

"I thought I had seen everything. The towns consumed by the trees, the people who no longer knew they were people, the landscapes twisted and broken beyond recognition. But today, I saw something new. Something that makes me think the worst is still to come."

"I had been walking for hours, trying to find some sign of civilization. The sky was dark, that unnatural red, but the air was strangely still. It's always quiet now, too quiet, like the world is holding its breath, waiting for something to happen. I hadn't seen any people for days, but I wasn't alone. I could feel something watching me."

"I came across a patch of forest, the trees black and twisted, their bark oozing with something that looked like sap but smelled like death. That's when I saw it—a rabbit, or what used to be a rabbit. At first, it didn't seem different, just… off. Its fur glowed faintly, like it was lit from within, a soft green light that pulsed in time with the tree's hum. I could feel the tree through it, feel it watching me through the creature's eyes."

"But when I moved closer, the rabbit turned toward me, and that's when I realized it wasn't an animal anymore. Its eyes were gone—replaced by black, empty voids that seemed to swallow the light. Its body was wrong, elongated, twisted, as if the tree had remade it in its own image. And then it bared its teeth—jagged, unnatural, far too many for a rabbit—and lunged."

"I barely managed to get away. It was fast, faster than any animal I'd ever seen. And I swear, it wasn't just reacting to me. It was hunting me, like it knew what I was. Like it hated me. I ran until I couldn't anymore, and when I looked back, the thing was gone, but the forest was alive with movement. I could see shapes in the trees, creatures that shouldn't exist, their eyes glowing in the darkness. The animals… they're not animals anymore. They're part of the tree. And they know we're here."

"I don't know how much longer I can survive like this. The trees are everywhere, and now even the wildlife has turned against us. The world isn't just changing. It's becoming something hostile, something alive in a way it never was before. The trees are remaking it in their own image, and I'm afraid that soon, there won't be anything left that's real. Only the nightmare."

Isaac's hands shook as he closed the diary. The Vagabond had encountered something new, something worse—wildlife that had been transformed by the tree's influence. Animals that were no longer just animals, but part of the corruption, their very bodies reshaped into something hostile, something dangerous.

Isaac stood up, his mind racing. The air in his house felt heavier, the shadows pressing down on him like a physical weight. He hadn't seen any animals around his home for weeks—at least, none that he recognized. But the idea that the wildlife, too, could be twisted by the tree... it made too much sense. Everything near the tree was changing—why wouldn't the animals?

A sudden noise from outside broke his thoughts. It was faint, but distinct—something moving in the yard. Isaac's pulse quickened. He grabbed the flashlight from the counter, though he wasn't sure what good it would do. He moved slowly to the window, peering out into the darkness beyond.

At first, he saw nothing but the tree, its massive branches swaying ever so slightly in the still, windless air. But then, at the edge of the yard, he noticed movement. A shape, low to the ground, slinking through the shadows. His breath caught in his throat as the creature stepped into the faint light cast by the blood-red moon.

It was a dog. Or, it had been a dog.

The creature's fur glowed faintly, a sickly green light that seemed to pulse in rhythm with the tree's hum. Its eyes, much like the rabbit described in the diary, were black and empty, voids that seemed to devour the light. Its body was gaunt, twisted unnaturally, with limbs that bent at disturbing angles. And then it turned its head toward Isaac, and he felt a chill shoot down his spine.

The dog—or whatever it had become—stared directly at him, as if it knew he was there. As if it could see him, even in the darkness. For a moment, they locked eyes, and Isaac felt a wave of nausea rise in his throat. There was something deeply wrong about the way the creature moved, the way it stood too still, as though it was waiting for him to make a move. But the worst part was the feeling in the back of his mind—the feeling that the tree was watching him through the creature's eyes.

He stepped back from the window, his heart pounding. The flashlight in his hand felt heavy and useless. He wasn't sure what to do. He couldn't leave. The world outside was too dangerous, too twisted by the tree's influence. But staying inside wasn't any better. The tree's presence was invading his mind, and now the creatures outside were changing, mutating into something worse than the aberrations—something that had once been familiar but was now completely alien.

Isaac sat down, trying to steady his breathing. The Vagabond's words echoed in his mind: *The animals... they're not animals anymore. They're part of the tree. And they know we're here.*

The dog was still out there, somewhere in the yard. He could feel it, sense it watching him from the shadows. But it wasn't alone. The Vagabond had seen more than one creature, and Isaac had no reason to believe that his home, his yard, was any different. The trees were corrupting everything—every living thing that came near them was being remade, twisted into something unnatural, something dangerous.

A soft scratching sound echoed from the back of the house, pulling Isaac from his thoughts. He froze, his eyes darting toward the door. The sound was faint, but steady, like claws dragging across wood.

It wasn't just one.

There were more of them.

Isaac's mind raced. He had no idea how many creatures were out there or what they wanted. He could feel the tree's influence pressing in on him, the hum growing louder, the air thicker. He was running out of time. The tree was taking everything—his mind, his world, and now even the animals that had once seemed harmless.

He flipped open the diary again, his eyes scanning the last lines of the Vagabond's entry. *The trees are remaking the world in their own image.*

Isaac gripped the edges of the notebook, his knuckles white. The Vagabond had seen what was happening long before Isaac had realized the full extent of it. The trees weren't just warping reality—they were reshaping the very nature of life itself. And now, that reshaping was coming for him.

Another scratch, louder this time, right outside the window.

Isaac looked around the room, searching for anything he could use to defend himself. But deep down, he knew the truth: there was no fighting this. The tree's influence was everywhere, warping everything it touched. And now, even the wildlife had become part of the nightmare.

The scratching stopped.

For a brief moment, there was silence.

And then the howling began.

CHAPTER 16

Desperation Spreads

The days had blended into one another. Isaac had stopped marking time, not because he didn't care, but because time itself seemed meaningless now. The blood-red moon hung perpetually in the sky, casting its eerie light over the landscape, and the tree in his yard continued to grow, twisting and pulsing with a life that defied understanding. The once-familiar world was falling apart around him, unraveling thread by thread.

He sat by the window, staring out at the desolate street. His neighborhood had been quiet for days, the silence broken only by the occasional distant howls of aberrations and the steady hum of the tree's influence. He had seen people—neighbors, passersby—driven mad by the tree's presence, wandering aimlessly until they disappeared into the wilderness. Some were claimed by the aberrations, while others simply vanished, consumed by the madness that now pervaded everything.

Isaac couldn't remember the last time he had seen a sign of normal life. The world was changing, evolving into something unrecognizable. It wasn't just the landscape that had been twisted by the tree's presence—humanity itself was fracturing. The news had gone silent, and the few radio transmissions Isaac still managed to catch were filled with fragmented stories of government collapse, military bases overrun, and entire cities swallowed by the aberrations and the trees' ever-spreading roots.

It was happening everywhere.

Cities that had once stood as symbols of strength and order—New York, London, Tokyo—were now battlegrounds, overrun by creatures born from the nightmare that the trees had unleashed. Governments that had once wielded power were crumbling, unable to fight back against something that defied logic. Entire regions were succumbing to madness, the people caught in an ever-worsening spiral of confusion and terror. Some tried to flee, but there was nowhere to go. The trees were spreading too fast, taking root in places that had once seemed safe.

Isaac had heard snippets of reports about cities not far from him. Baltimore had been overrun, its streets filled with creatures that roamed freely, hunting anything that moved. Philadelphia had gone dark, and the military outposts around it had fallen silent. Even Washington, D.C., had become a shadow of its former self, the government's last desperate attempts at controlling the situation falling apart as the trees continued to spread and mutate everything in their path.

He had seen it in his own neighborhood, where the tree had taken over his yard, warping the very air around it. The aberrations that emerged from the tree were becoming more aggressive, venturing further from its roots, and the natural world had twisted in response. The creatures were no longer just mindless hunters—they were evolving, adapting to the new reality the tree had created.

Isaac stood up from his spot by the window, feeling the weight of the world pressing down on him. The desperation was spreading like wildfire, consuming everything in its path. People were either killed by the aberrations or driven mad by the tree's influence. The few that survived were clinging to whatever scraps of hope they could find, but those scraps were dwindling fast.

He looked out at the street again. The ground around the tree was cracked and warped, the very laws of physics seeming to break down in its presence. Objects seemed to bend and twist as they neared the tree, time itself stretching and snapping in ways that made no sense. The once-stable reality he had known was unraveling, and there was nothing anyone could do to stop it.

The Research Group's Struggle

Far from Isaac's isolated nightmare, the scientists at **GRIAP** were watching the same thing unfold on a global scale. The underground facility was abuzz with frantic activity, the tension in the air palpable as Dr. Isabel Martinez and her team raced against the clock to understand what was happening. They had been studying the trees for months, gathering data, running simulations, trying to find some way to combat the spread. But now, it seemed that every discovery they made only led to more questions.

The trees were evolving.

Martinez stood in front of a large monitor, her eyes fixed on the data scrolling across the screen. Satellite imagery from across the world showed the spread of the trees—each one growing faster, stronger, more adaptive. They were no longer just biological anomalies. The trees were becoming something else, something that defied the very fabric of reality. The gravitational anomalies near the trees had grown more severe, and now, even the laws of physics seemed to be breaking down.

"Look at this," Dr. David Johansson said, pointing to a graph on the monitor. "We've been tracking the electromagnetic fields around the trees for weeks, but now... now it's off the charts. The trees are emitting something—some kind of energy we can't fully measure. And it's not just affecting the environment. It's warping space-time itself."

Martinez frowned, her mind racing as she tried to make sense of the data. "The aberrations are becoming more aggressive too," she said, her voice tight with frustration. "Every report we've received from the field indicates that the creatures are adapting to our attempts to understand them. They're evolving."

Dr. Elaine Parson, who had been monitoring the psychological effects of the trees, spoke up. "It's not just the creatures. It's the people. Tree Psychosis is spreading faster than we anticipated. The closer people get to the trees, the faster their minds break down. We've lost more field teams in the last month than in the entire first half of this crisis. It's like the trees are learning how to break people."

Martinez nodded grimly. "It's as if the trees are tapping into something deeper, something beyond our understanding. They're not just changing the world around them—they're changing reality itself. And we're running out of time."

The team had been studying the trees' influence on time and space for weeks, but the anomalies were becoming more extreme, more unpredictable. In some areas, time seemed to stretch and contract at random, while in others, gravity fluctuated wildly, making movement near the trees almost impossible. Objects that neared the trees would warp and bend, their shapes twisting in ways that defied the laws of physics.

Martinez's mind raced as she stared at the data. The trees were evolving, adapting to their environment in ways that no one could have predicted. And with each adaptation, they became stronger, more integrated into the fabric of the world.

But what was driving this evolution? And how could they stop it?

"We need to focus on the core of the tree," Martinez said, turning to the rest of the team. "The roots are the key. Every time we've sent teams into the tree zones, the roots seem to be the epicenter of the anomalies. If we can figure out what's happening at the core, we might be able to stop it."

Johansson shook his head, his expression grim. "That's easier said than done. Every attempt to get close to the core has failed. The aberrations guard the area fiercely, and the gravitational and temporal distortions make it nearly impossible to get close without losing people. We've already lost too many."

Martinez clenched her fists, feeling the weight of the situation pressing down on her. The trees were evolving, the aberrations were growing stronger, and reality itself was breaking down around them. But they couldn't give up. They had to find a way to stop this before it was too late.

"We don't have a choice," she said, her voice steady. "We need to find a way to neutralize the trees. If we don't, there won't be a world left to save."

Desperate Measures

Back in his home, Isaac could feel the growing pressure of the tree's presence. The air around him felt heavier with each passing day, the ground shifting beneath his feet as reality twisted and warped. The world outside was falling apart, and Isaac knew he couldn't stay here much longer. The aberrations were becoming bolder, venturing closer to his home, and the tree's influence was seeping into his mind more deeply than ever.

He flipped through the pages of his notebook, trying to hold on to some semblance of control. He had been documenting everything—the changes in the environment, the creatures he had seen, the way time and space seemed to bend around the tree. But no matter how much he wrote, no matter how many observations he made, the truth was becoming painfully clear: the world was collapsing, and he was powerless to stop it.

Isaac stood up and walked to the window, his eyes scanning the street outside. The once-familiar neighborhood was a wasteland now, the ground cracked and twisted, the sky an eternal red. In the distance, he could see the twisted forms of aberrations moving through the wreckage, their bodies shifting and warping as they prowled the streets.

The desperation was spreading. People were either dead, driven mad, or hiding in whatever remnants of safety they could find. And Isaac was no different. He was clinging to the last threads of sanity, trying to understand what was happening, but the truth was slipping further and further out of reach.

The world was changing, evolving into something unrecognizable. The trees were adapting, the aberrations were growing stronger, and the very fabric of reality was unraveling. And Isaac knew, deep down, that there was no going back.

The nightmare was just beginning.

CHAPTER 17

Underground Resistance —Morality in Conflict

Isaac sat by the window, staring out at the shifting, broken landscape beyond his home. His world had shrunk to this small, crumbling space, the view dominated by the massive tree in his yard, its gnarled branches twisting up into the blood-red sky. The hum of the tree filled the air, vibrating through his bones, making it difficult to think. Days, or maybe weeks, had passed since he had last heard any news. The world outside his house seemed so distant now, consumed by madness and destruction.

But today, there was something new—a figure moving through the street. Isaac hadn't seen another person in days, perhaps even longer. He felt a surge of both hope and fear as he watched the lone figure approach. They were moving cautiously, as if aware of the dangers lurking in the shadows, but determined.

Isaac stood up, pressing his face closer to the window, his heart pounding. Was this person lost? Were they running from the aberrations, or had they come here for a reason? He debated whether to stay hidden or make himself known, but a part of him, the part that still clung to the need for human connection, won out.

He cracked open the door slightly, just enough to let his voice carry. "Hey!" he called, his voice weak and hoarse from disuse. The figure froze, their head snapping in his direction, eyes scanning the area cautiously.

Isaac stepped out onto the porch, still keeping his distance, his hands raised to show he wasn't a threat. "Are you… are you with the resistance?"

The figure hesitated for a moment, then nodded slowly. "Yeah," the man said, his voice low. "Name's Damon. You heard of us?"

"I've heard rumors," Isaac replied, stepping closer but still keeping an eye on the surrounding area. He had grown paranoid, constantly on alert for the aberrations that now prowled the streets. "You're fighting back, right? Trying to stop all this?"

Damon scoffed, but there was no humor in his voice. "Trying. But it's a losing battle."

Isaac motioned for Damon to come closer, glancing around nervously. "You should come inside. It's not safe out here."

Damon hesitated, glancing at the tree in Isaac's yard before nodding and following him inside. Once the door was closed, Isaac felt a strange mix of relief and tension. It had been so long since he'd spoken to anyone, but Damon's presence was unsettling. There was something about him—a heaviness in his demeanor, a bitterness that Isaac could see in his eyes.

Damon looked around Isaac's disheveled home, taking in the sight of notebooks scattered across tables, maps marked with hastily drawn notes, and a small radio still faintly humming static. "You've been holed up here this whole time?"

Isaac nodded, sitting down at the kitchen table. "I haven't had much of a choice. The tree… it's changed everything around here. The aberrations, the way the ground moves… I don't know how much longer I can stay here."

Damon sat across from him, pulling a flask from his coat and taking a long drink before speaking. "You're not the only one trapped. The world's falling apart faster than we can handle. We've been trying to fight, but it's like every time we think we've got a plan, the trees change the rules."

Isaac leaned forward, desperate for any information about what was happening beyond his small corner of the world. "But you're fighting. How are you doing it? What's the plan?"

Damon sighed, running a hand through his hair. "There's no plan anymore. Not really. We started out trying to take down nests of aberrations, clear out the smaller trees, help survivors... but the trees are spreading faster than we can destroy them. Kellar's been leading us, but things are falling apart. We've lost too many people, and now..."

He trailed off, staring down at his hands as if the weight of everything was too much to bear.

"And now?" Isaac pressed.

Damon looked up, his eyes filled with anger and something darker—resignation. "Now we're turning against each other."

Internal Conflict in the Resistance

The **Underground Resistance** had been Kellar's creation—a group of fighters, scavengers, and survivors who had banded together with the shared goal of fighting back against the trees and the aberrations. At first, they had been united by a common purpose: survival. They had struck at the heart of aberration nests, using guerrilla tactics to destroy smaller trees and rescue as many civilians as they could. But as the trees grew stronger, and the aberrations more aggressive, the losses had mounted.

Kellar had always been a soldier, but after watching the world crumble around him, his bitterness had only deepened. The people in power—governments, military leaders, bureaucrats—had failed to stop the spread. They had clung to traditional tactics and strategies, believing that brute force could contain the threat. But Kellar knew better. The aberrations didn't follow the rules of warfare, and neither did the trees. The more the resistance fought, the more it became clear that the rules of reality itself were being rewritten.

Now, Kellar's once clear mission had blurred, and the group was fracturing under the pressure.

"There's no leadership anymore," Damon said, shaking his head. "Half the group still believes in Kellar's mission—taking the fight to the aberrations, blowing up nests, striking where we can. But some of the others... they're starting to think it's pointless."

Isaac frowned. "What do you mean?"

"They want to stop fighting the aberrations directly," Damon explained, his voice laced with frustration. "Instead, they want to go after what's left of the governments. They think the people in power are too afraid to take the kind of risks we need. So they've started sabotaging military efforts, government bases... anywhere they think the authorities are still in control."

Isaac's stomach turned at the thought. "They're attacking their own people?"

Damon nodded, bitterness in his voice. "They don't see it that way. To them, the governments are just part of the problem now. They're too weak, too slow. Kellar doesn't trust them anymore, and the more desperate things get, the more reckless he's becoming."

Isaac could hear the frustration in Damon's voice, but he could also sense the underlying fear. It wasn't just about the fight anymore—it was about survival, and the resistance was coming apart at the seams. The pressure of fighting an impossible war was breaking them, turning their once-noble mission into something darker, more dangerous.

"Some of us still believe in the original goal," Damon continued. "But there's less of us now. Every mission we lose more people. And Kellar... he's changed. He's angry, but it's more than that. He's stopped caring about the costs."

Isaac shook his head, trying to make sense of it all. "But what choice do you have? If you stop fighting..."

"We die," Damon finished for him, his voice hollow. "But if we keep fighting like this, we die too. Kellar's losing himself, and the rest of us... we're caught in the middle. We don't trust the government to fix this, but we can't keep fighting like we're invincible. We're not."

Isaac felt the weight of Damon's words settle over him. It was clear that the resistance was no longer the beacon of hope it had once seemed. The world had changed, twisted by the trees, and the people who had once stood against it were being pulled into the same darkness.

For a moment, Isaac didn't know what to say. He had spent so much time isolated in his home, trying to make sense of the madness around him, that he hadn't fully grasped how far the world had fallen. But hearing Damon's story, hearing how even the resistance was fracturing under the pressure, made it clear: the world was breaking in ways he couldn't have imagined.

"They're not going to stop, are they?" Isaac asked quietly.

Damon shook his head. "Not until there's nothing left."

Morality in Question

Damon stayed with Isaac for a while longer, sharing stories of the resistance's struggles, the victories they had fought so hard for, and the losses that haunted them. As they spoke, it became clear to Isaac that the resistance was no longer just fighting the trees and the aberrations—they were fighting themselves, torn between the desire to survive and the growing bitterness that came with every defeat.

Isaac could see it in Damon's eyes, the same look he had seen in the mirror so many times. The desperation. The exhaustion. The creeping sense that no matter what they did, it wouldn't be enough.

But there was something else too. Beneath the anger and the fear, there was still a flicker of hope. Damon still believed in what the resistance had stood for, even if it was falling apart now. And that hope, fragile as it was, was something Isaac clung to.

As Damon left, disappearing back into the twisted streets, Isaac sat in the silence of his home, the hum of the tree louder than ever. The world was collapsing, and the resistance—the one group he had hoped might turn the tide—was falling apart from within.

But somewhere, buried beneath the despair, was the belief that people could still fight back. That there was still a chance.

Isaac wasn't sure if it was true.

But it was all he had left.

CHAPTER 18
The Vagabond's Diary —Growing Despair

Isaac's world had been reduced to a constant cycle of fear, confusion, and isolation. The tree in his yard had become an unrelenting presence, a looming reminder of the collapse happening all around him. His mind was fraying at the edges, unraveling like so many others he had seen lost to the tree's influence. The aberrations prowled the streets, and the natural world—what was left of it—was warping into something far more dangerous. Each day felt like a battle to hold onto reality, a fight to stay grounded while the rest of the world spun out of control.

Sitting in the fading light of his home, Isaac reached for the **Vagabond's Diary** again. The strange, fragmented accounts had become his lifeline, a dark mirror to his own experience. Each entry echoed his thoughts and fears, as if the Vagabond had walked this path before him, experiencing the same creeping madness that threatened to consume him now. With trembling fingers, Isaac flipped to the next entry, feeling the weight of the words before he even began to read.

Vagabond's Diary - Fourth Entry

"I thought I had seen the worst of it. The trees, the people lost to their nightmares, the aberrations stalking the streets. But now I know I was wrong. The worst is still coming. It's everywhere now—this creeping, insidious thing that we can't stop. We can't escape it. And it's changing everything."

"I left the last town days ago, walking through what used to be countryside. But the land isn't the same anymore. It's hostile. I can feel it—everything is watching, everything is alive in a way it wasn't before. The trees have spread their roots deep into the earth, and they're infecting everything they touch."

"The ground is hard to walk on, like it's shifting beneath my feet. Thorns grow out of nowhere, sharp and deadly, twisting toward me as I pass. I try to stay on the paths, but the paths change. It's like the trees are playing with me, testing me, seeing how far I can go before I give in. I've seen plants that glow in the dark, flowers that hum like the trees, their petals razor-sharp, slicing through the air if I get too close."

"I'm not alone. I've seen others—people wandering like I am, but they don't last long. I've watched them get too close to the plants, seen the vines wrap around their legs and pull them down. The land itself is turning against us. It doesn't want us here. It's rejecting us."

"I don't know how much longer I can keep going. The trees are everywhere. Entire regions have collapsed, towns and cities swallowed up by the roots, the thorns, the plants. There's no safety anymore. The air feels thicker, like I'm breathing in the tree's influence. Every breath feels like it's pulling me deeper into this nightmare. I keep walking, but there's nowhere left to go."

Isaac swallowed hard, the words resonating with a depth he hadn't expected. The Vagabond's despair was palpable, the helplessness and exhaustion seeping through every sentence. The once peaceful world had become a hostile, living entity, reshaped by the trees' influence. The land itself had turned against them, attacking those who dared to approach. Thorns, twisting vines, and unnatural growths had become new weapons in the trees' arsenal.

The Vagabond's experience felt eerily familiar. Isaac had seen it firsthand in his own yard, watching as the ground seemed to shift beneath him, the air growing thicker, harder to breathe, as if the tree was choking the life out of everything around it. He had noticed how the once simple plants—the grass, the flowers, the bushes—had become something else. The grass had turned brittle, sharp enough to cut his skin if he wasn't careful, and the flowers now twisted toward him as if aware of his presence. The environment was no longer just dangerous—it was actively hostile, just like the Vagabond had described.

Isaac's eyes flicked to the window, staring out at the tree as its branches twisted in the crimson sky. The hum was louder today, vibrating through his entire body, making it hard to think. He could feel the weight of the air, the strange density that made each breath feel like an effort. And just beyond the tree, in the shadows of the yard, he saw movement.

Something was crawling, slow and deliberate, moving through the twisted plants that had overtaken his once tidy garden. Isaac's heart raced as he watched, his mind racing back to the Vagabond's words. The land is alive, rejecting us. The plants don't just sit idly by—they attack, they kill.

Isaac grabbed his flashlight and slowly stepped closer to the window, trying to get a better look. The shadows flickered as the figure moved closer to the house, slinking low to the ground. It was hard to tell if it was human or something else entirely. His pulse quickened, and his mouth went dry. The tree's influence had spread far beyond the house, far beyond what was visible. He knew now that there was nowhere safe, nowhere untouched.

He thought back to the diary, to the Vagabond's growing despair. Every step the Vagabond had taken had been met with more resistance, more hostility from the world around them. The plants, the land, the air—it had all turned against them. Isaac couldn't shake the feeling that he was on the same path, that no matter what he did, the tree was going to consume him too.

The scratching at the back door pulled him out of his thoughts, and Isaac jumped, his nerves shot. He moved toward the sound cautiously, gripping the flashlight like a weapon. The sound grew louder, more insistent, and Isaac's heart pounded in his chest as he reached the door.

Slowly, he opened it a crack, peering into the dim light of the yard. Nothing. He stepped out, his breath shallow, and turned the corner of the house. And then he saw it—one of the twisted plants, its thorns moving as if alive, its vines reaching out toward him. The ground beneath it shifted, the roots spreading like fingers through the dirt.

Isaac stepped back, his pulse racing. The land was alive, just like the Vagabond had said. It was watching him, hunting him, waiting for him to make a mistake.

He hurried back inside, slamming the door behind him, his mind spinning. The tree wasn't just a passive force of nature—it was actively changing the world around it, turning the very environment into a hostile, predatory landscape. The Vagabond had been right. There was no escaping this.

Vagabond's Diary - Fourth Entry (Continued)

"I've tried to avoid the trees, but it's impossible. The thorns reach out when you least expect it, and the ground shifts like it's alive. The air gets thicker the closer I get to the trees, like it's trying to pull me in, suffocate me. I've seen people lose themselves to it—walking into the thorns like they don't even see them, letting the vines wrap around them without a fight. It's like the tree takes their minds first, then their bodies."

"I don't know how long I can keep going like this. I'm tired. So tired. Every step feels heavier. Every breath feels like it's pulling me deeper into this nightmare. I keep telling myself there's hope somewhere, that I just need to find it, but it's getting harder to believe that now."

"The world is changing, and I don't think there's a way back. The trees are spreading too fast. The aberrations are becoming more aggressive, more aware.

They're not just hunting us—they're driving us toward the trees. It's like they know what the trees want, and they're doing its bidding."

"I'm afraid I'll lose myself soon. The whispers are getting louder. The shadows are moving when they shouldn't. And the thorns... they're getting closer."

Isaac closed the diary, his hands trembling. The Vagabond's despair was overwhelming, their words heavy with the realization that the world was collapsing in ways no one could have imagined. The land itself was no longer a safe haven—it was an enemy, twisted and remade by the tree's influence. And now, Isaac knew, he was facing the same fate. The plants in his own yard, the shifting ground, the vines that seemed to move on their own—it was all connected, part of the tree's expanding reach.

He could feel the same despair creeping into his own mind. The idea that there was no escape, that the tree would eventually consume everything, was becoming harder to ignore. The Vagabond had walked through a collapsing world, and Isaac was right behind them, following the same path, facing the same nightmare.

Isaac stared out at the twisted landscape, the trees, the thorns, the unnatural sky. The world was hostile now, and it felt like it was rejecting him, pushing him deeper into the madness. There was no going back. And there was nowhere left to go.

CHAPTER 19
Inquisition's Involvement

Isaac sat at his kitchen table, hands wrapped around a mug of cold coffee. His eyes, bloodshot and heavy with exhaustion, darted between the cracked window and the **Vagabond's Diary**, open in front of him. The entries had been a grim reflection of his own experiences, each one confirming what he already feared: the world was changing, and there was no escaping it. The tree in his yard was growing stronger, its roots creeping further into his thoughts, its branches casting twisted shadows across his home.

He had long accepted that he was isolated—cut off from what little remained of society. The radio was dead, and the few broadcasts he had caught were fragmented at best, telling stories of governments falling, cities being consumed by the trees, and the unstoppable spread of aberrations. Each day, the world seemed to shrink further, drawing closer to the nightmare that the Vagabond had warned about.

But today was different. For the first time in weeks, Isaac wasn't alone.

The two figures sitting across from him were shrouded in a strange sense of authority, but it was unlike any he had seen before. They didn't wear the uniforms of soldiers or government agents. Instead, they were dressed in long, dark coats, their expressions unreadable, their presence unsettling. They called themselves **Inquisitors**, and they had arrived with promises of answers—but the answers they offered came with unsettling implications.

Isaac couldn't stop staring at the woman in front of him. She had introduced herself simply as **Lydia**, but there was something ancient in her eyes, something that told Isaac that this was no ordinary person. Her companion, a tall, stern-faced man named **Vernon**, had been silent for most of the conversation, his sharp gaze observing everything with a cold precision.

"We've been watching you," Lydia said, her voice calm but with an underlying intensity that made Isaac's skin prickle. "You've survived this long, alone, near one of the largest trees we've seen. That's no small feat."

Isaac felt a chill run down his spine. "I'm not sure what you're talking about," he replied, his voice rough from disuse. "I've just been… surviving."

Lydia exchanged a glance with Vernon, her lips curling into a slight smile that didn't reach her eyes. "You're more than a survivor. The tree should have claimed you by now. Its influence should have driven you mad, like so many others. But here you are—still lucid, still holding on."

Isaac's heart pounded in his chest. He had felt the tree's pull, the constant hum in his mind, the nightmares that blurred the line between reality and madness. But he had fought it, clinging to his sanity with every ounce of strength he had left. Still, the idea that he had been watched—that these people knew more about him than he knew about them—was deeply unsettling.

"Who are you?" Isaac asked, his voice tinged with both curiosity and fear. "What do you want from me?"

Lydia's gaze softened, though it was clear that she was still carefully measuring her words. "We are part of an ancient order known as the **Inquisition**. Our purpose is to combat threats like this—threats that defy the natural order of the world."

"The trees?" Isaac asked, his mind racing. "You know what they are?"

Vernon, who had been silent until now, finally spoke. His voice was deep and commanding. "The trees are not a new phenomenon. They have ancient origins, dating back to times long forgotten by most of humanity. This isn't the first time they've appeared, though it is the first time they've emerged on such a global scale."

Isaac's mind reeled at the thought. The trees had been here before? "Why now?" he asked, his voice barely above a whisper. "Why are they back?"

"The world has changed," Lydia replied. "The balance has been disrupted, and the trees have returned to reclaim what they once sought. They are more than just biological entities—they are tied to something deeper, something far older than anything our modern science can explain."

Isaac felt the weight of her words settle over him. He had known, deep down, that the trees were more than just strange plants. They had an intelligence, a purpose that went beyond mere growth. But to hear that they were tied to ancient forces, to something beyond his comprehension, sent a shiver down his spine.

"But how do you know this?" Isaac asked, trying to wrap his mind around the enormity of what Lydia was saying.

Lydia's smile returned, colder this time. "The Inquisition has existed for centuries, tasked with protecting the world from forces like these. We've seen the trees before, though never on this scale. We have knowledge that has been passed down through generations—knowledge that combines both ancient sorcery and lost technologies, tools that were once used to fight these very entities."

Isaac's hands tightened around the edge of the table. "Sorcery?" The word felt strange on his tongue. "You're telling me that magic is real?"

"Heretical sorcery," Vernon corrected, his tone sharp. "Not the kind of magic you hear about in fairy tales, but a dangerous, forbidden power that we have harnessed for one purpose: to stop the trees from spreading. Combined with ancient technologies that were lost to time, it's the only way we stand a chance against them."

Isaac's mind was spinning. The idea that sorcery, heresy, and ancient technology were involved in this nightmare was overwhelming. But there was one thing that mattered more than anything else. "Can you stop them?" he asked, his voice desperate. "Can you stop the trees?"

Lydia's smile faltered, and her eyes darkened. "We can slow them. We've been working in secret, targeting the smaller trees, using our methods to contain the spread. But this... this is bigger than anything we've faced before. The trees are evolving, adapting faster than we anticipated."

Isaac swallowed hard. "Evolving? What do you mean?"

"The trees aren't just growing," Lydia explained. "They're learning. They've started adapting to the environment, changing the way they interact with reality itself. Your research group has likely noticed the anomalies—the way gravity shifts, the way time warps near the trees."

Isaac's heart skipped a beat at the mention of the research group. He had heard about them—scientists who were trying to understand the trees, working from deep within underground facilities. "The research group," Isaac said, his voice quickening. "They're studying the trees. Do they know what's happening?"

Lydia's expression darkened. "They've made progress, but their efforts are being sabotaged."

Isaac's brow furrowed. "Sabotaged? By who?"

"The Inquisition has infiltrators within the group," Vernon said flatly. "We needed to ensure that their findings didn't reach the wrong hands. The governments and military are too reliant on traditional methods—methods that will fail against the trees. We couldn't let the public learn too much, too soon."

Isaac felt a rush of anger rise in his chest. "You've been stopping them from finding a solution? People are dying, and you're playing politics?"

Vernon's eyes flashed with cold anger. "This is bigger than you can understand. The public isn't ready for the truth. If they knew what the trees really were, there would be chaos. Panic. The world is already on the brink of collapse—we can't afford to let it fall any faster."

Isaac stood up, his fists clenched. "And what about the people already falling? What about the towns and cities that have been consumed? The research group might have found something—something that could help."

Lydia raised a hand, her voice calm but firm. "We're not here to argue, Isaac. We're here to offer you a choice."

Isaac stared at her, his pulse racing. "A choice?"

Lydia nodded. "You've survived this long for a reason. The tree in your yard is one of the oldest, one of the strongest. Its roots run deep into the earth, and it's tied to something far more powerful than you can imagine. We need your help."

"My help?" Isaac scoffed, shaking his head. "What could I possibly do?"

Lydia leaned forward, her voice dropping to a whisper. "You're closer to the truth than you realize. The roots—the very heart of the tree—is the key to stopping all of this. If we can destroy the core, we can stop the spread. But we need someone who can withstand the tree's influence, someone who can get close enough to the heart without losing themselves."

Isaac's mind raced. The roots. The core. The research group had been focusing on the same thing, trying to understand how the trees were connected to the fabric of reality. And now, the Inquisition was telling him that the answer was buried deep within the tree's ancient roots.

He felt the weight of their words settle over him, the enormity of what they were asking sinking in.

"I don't know if I can," Isaac whispered, the fear in his voice undeniable. "I've barely survived this long."

Lydia stood, her eyes softening as she placed a hand on his shoulder. "We all have our part to play. The tree has ancient origins, yes, but that doesn't mean it can't be stopped. You're stronger than you think, Isaac. And we'll be with you every step of the way."

Isaac swallowed hard, the fear and doubt swirling in his chest. But somewhere deep inside, there was something else—a flicker of determination.

He had come this far. He had survived. And if there was a chance, no matter how small, to stop the trees, he had to take it.

For the first time in weeks, Isaac felt like he had a purpose.

CHAPTER 20
Resistance's Major Losses

Kellar paced the length of the abandoned factory, his boots echoing off the cracked concrete floor. The resistance's makeshift base was a far cry from what it had been just months ago. The space, once bustling with activity—fighters prepping for missions, tech experts repairing scavenged equipment, and strategists drawing up plans—now felt like a tomb. It was quiet, far too quiet, save for the distant hum of machinery and the nervous murmurs of the few remaining resistance members. The group had been whittled down to a shadow of its former self, their numbers devastated by failed strikes and relentless battles against the aberrations.

Tonight's mission was different, though. Kellar had promised that. He had convinced what was left of the team that this strike, this one desperate attempt to deal a blow to the enemy, would be the turning point. But deep down, even Kellar was beginning to doubt his own words. Too many had died. Too many missions had gone wrong. And tonight... something felt off.

The warehouse doors screeched as Damon entered, looking grim. His face was pale, eyes shadowed with exhaustion, but there was still a spark of determination burning in him. He crossed the room and stopped in front of Kellar, holding a small, worn-out tablet in his hand.

"It's ready," Damon said quietly, handing the device to Kellar. "The tech guys say the EMP will work, but... you know the risks."

Kellar nodded, barely glancing at the screen. The EMP, scavenged from an old military base and retrofitted with bits of salvaged technology, was their last hope. The aberrations were growing stronger, more numerous, and the usual tactics of explosives and guerrilla strikes were proving ineffective. The resistance had managed to piece together a working EMP device, theorizing that it could disrupt the strange electromagnetic field that surrounded the aberrations, at least temporarily disabling them and giving the team a chance to strike.

But the plan was risky. They'd never tested the tech on a large scale, and there was no guarantee it would work. Worse, if the device malfunctioned, it could backfire, potentially taking out the resistance members in the process. Still, Kellar had pushed for the mission, driven by desperation and the desire to hit the aberrations where it hurt. They were running out of time and options.

"I know the risks," Kellar said, his voice hard. "But it's the only shot we've got."

Damon nodded, though his expression was tight with worry. "The team's ready, but… I'm not sure how much faith they've got in this. We've been burned before."

Kellar stopped pacing and looked Damon in the eyes. "We don't have the luxury of doubt. Either we hit them hard tonight, or we lose everything."

Damon sighed but said nothing more. He understood the stakes, even if the others didn't. The aberrations were growing in numbers, and the trees were spreading across the landscape like a plague. Each day they delayed meant more cities falling, more people dying. If this mission didn't work, the resistance would crumble completely.

Kellar watched as the remaining resistance members geared up, their faces tense and pale in the dim light of the factory. He could feel the weight of their hope and fear pressing down on him. It was a heavy burden, but Kellar had no choice but to carry it.

The Strike Begins

The mission took them to the outskirts of what had once been a bustling industrial city, now overrun by the trees and the twisted aberrations that patrolled the streets. The air was thick with the scent of decay, the buildings crumbling under the weight of the trees' spreading roots. Kellar's team moved through the streets, staying low and silent, their eyes scanning the darkness for any sign of the creatures.

The target was a large nest of aberrations—one of the biggest they had seen. The creatures had been congregating near an old power plant, and intelligence suggested that the plant's electromagnetic field had somehow attracted them. The plan was to hit them with the EMP, disrupting the field and hopefully disabling the aberrations long enough for the team to plant explosives and take out the nest.

As they approached the power plant, the tension among the team was palpable. The air felt heavy, oppressive, as if the trees themselves were watching, waiting. Kellar could feel the weight of it pressing down on him, but he forced himself to focus. There was no room for fear. Not now.

They reached the perimeter of the plant, crouching behind the rusted remains of an old fence. The aberrations were everywhere—dark, hulking figures moving through the shadows, their many eyes glowing faintly in the dim light. Kellar's grip tightened on his rifle as he surveyed the scene.

"This is it," Kellar whispered to the group. "We move fast, hit them hard, and get out. Damon, you're on the EMP. Everyone else, be ready to plant the charges as soon as it goes off."

Damon nodded, his fingers hovering over the tablet that controlled the EMP device. The team waited, their breath held, as Damon activated the countdown.

The device began to hum, a low, vibrating sound that seemed to reverberate through the ground. For a moment, everything was still. The aberrations didn't seem to notice, their twisted forms continuing to move through the ruined plant. Kellar's heart pounded in his chest as the countdown neared its end.

3... 2... 1...

The EMP exploded in a flash of light and sound, sending a shockwave through the air that rippled out across the power plant. The aberrations froze, their bodies twitching and convulsing as the electromagnetic field around them was disrupted. For a brief, shining moment, it worked. The creatures were disabled, their grotesque limbs jerking spasmodically as the field short-circuited.

"Now!" Kellar shouted, signaling to the team. They moved quickly, rushing forward to plant the explosives around the nest, their movements quick and efficient. For the first time in weeks, Kellar felt a surge of hope. Maybe this would work. Maybe they could actually win this one.

But then, something went wrong.

The EMP device, still humming with residual energy, began to spark violently. Damon's eyes widened in horror as the tablet in his hands started to smoke. "Kellar!" he shouted, his voice filled with panic. "The device—it's malfunctioning!"

Before Kellar could respond, the EMP let out a second, uncontrolled shockwave, much stronger than the first. The ground trembled beneath their feet as the pulse rippled outward, catching both the aberrations and the resistance members in its path. Kellar felt the shockwave slam into him, knocking the breath from his lungs and sending him sprawling to the ground.

The air was filled with a high-pitched ringing, and Kellar struggled to push himself to his feet, his vision blurred. Around him, the rest of the team lay scattered, some unconscious, others writhing in pain. But worse, far worse, were the aberrations.

The creatures, though still affected by the EMP, were adapting. Their bodies, twisted and grotesque, were jerking violently as they absorbed the pulse, their movements becoming erratic, more frenzied. The EMP, instead of disabling them, seemed to have triggered some kind of reaction—an evolution.

"Kellar!" Damon screamed, pulling himself to his feet, his face pale with fear. "They're coming back!"

The aberrations, now even more aggressive, began to lurch forward, their eyes glowing with an unnatural light. The team, disoriented and weakened by the malfunctioning EMP, had no chance.

"Kellar, we have to go!" Damon shouted again, grabbing Kellar's arm and pulling him back. "We're not going to make it!"

But Kellar's mind was blank with shock. Everything had gone wrong. The mission had failed. He had led his team into a trap of their own making, and now the aberrations were coming for them.

The creatures moved fast, their bodies twisting and contorting as they surged toward the resistance fighters. One by one, the team members fell, their screams piercing the night as the aberrations tore through them.

Kellar stumbled backward, his vision blurring with tears and rage. He had promised them victory. He had promised them hope. But now, there was only death.

Aftermath

By the time Kellar and Damon reached the outskirts of the power plant, only a handful of resistance fighters were left. The rest were dead, their bodies strewn across the broken landscape, their faces twisted in agony.

Kellar stood in the ruins, his hands shaking, his heart pounding with grief and rage. He had failed them. The mission was supposed to be their turning point, the strike that would push the aberrations back. But instead, it had been a catastrophe.

Damon limped over to him, his face pale, his voice barely a whisper. "What now?"

Kellar didn't respond. He couldn't. His mind was numb with the weight of what had happened. The resistance was broken. Their numbers were decimated, their hope shattered.

They couldn't fight this alone anymore.

"We need help," Damon said, his voice shaking. "Kellar, we have to go to them."

Kellar turned to look at him, his eyes hollow. "The Inquisition?"

Damon nodded. "It's the only way. We can't keep doing this. We need their resources, their knowledge. If we don't… there won't be anything left."

Kellar clenched his fists, the bitterness and rage swirling inside him. He had resisted going to the Inquisition for so long, refusing to trust anyone outside of the resistance. But now, with so few fighters left, with everything falling apart, he had no choice.

"We'll find them," Kellar said, his voice a low growl. "And when we do, we'll make sure they help us."

Damon nodded, but there was no relief in his expression. Only the shared understanding that this was the end of the resistance as they had known it.

They had lost everything. And now, their only hope lay in the hands of an organization they didn't trust.

Catastrophic Attack on Research Base

The tension inside the **Global Research Initiative on Anomalous Phenomena (GRIAP)** was thick enough to cut with a knife. For weeks, Dr. Isabel Martinez and her team had been working under the constant threat of attack. The anomalies caused by the tree's influence had become more frequent, and reports of aberrations swarming nearby cities were increasing daily. The team had grown accustomed to the rumbling of distant explosions, the crackling of radios, and the hurried conversations that spoke of crumbling defenses.

But none of that had prepared them for this moment.

The base was buzzing with activity as researchers rushed to compile the latest data, hastily analyzing the tree's influence on the local environment. Dr. Martinez stood in front of a large monitor displaying complex graphs and charts, her fingers drumming nervously on the table. The recent data showed something alarming: the tree was evolving faster than they had anticipated. Its roots were growing deeper, intertwining with the fabric of reality itself, and the gravitational distortions near its epicenter were becoming more extreme.

"We need to move faster," she muttered to herself, her eyes darting across the data. "We're running out of time."

Dr. David Johansson, the team's physicist, leaned over her shoulder, pointing to a specific section of the graph. "These fluctuations... they're accelerating.

If this keeps up, we'll lose our window to understand the core. The distortions will be too severe to get close."

Martinez nodded, her mind racing. They had uncovered a critical piece of the puzzle: the tree's roots were the key to its power, and if they could find a way to sever that connection, they might be able to stop the tree's spread. But the more they studied the tree, the more dangerous it became. The aberrations were becoming more aggressive, the environment more hostile.

And now, they were about to lose everything.

A low rumble shook the base, sending a tremor through the floor. Martinez froze, her heart skipping a beat. The room fell silent for a moment as everyone exchanged nervous glances.

"Did you feel that?" Johansson asked, his voice barely above a whisper.

Before anyone could answer, the alarms blared to life, filling the air with a deafening wail. Red lights flashed across the walls as the base's emergency protocols kicked in. The sound of boots pounding against the metal floor echoed through the corridors as security personnel scrambled into position.

Martinez's stomach dropped. "No," she whispered, fear creeping into her voice. "Not now. Not here."

One of the technicians rushed toward her, his face pale and drenched in sweat. "Dr. Martinez, we've got movement outside. It's the aberrations—they're swarming the perimeter."

Martinez's mind raced. They had been expecting an attack, but not this soon. The research base was deep underground, fortified against most threats, but the aberrations had been adapting, growing more intelligent with each passing day. And now, they had come for the heart of the research operation.

"Secure the data!" Martinez barked, her voice cutting through the rising panic. "We can't lose this. Gather everything you can and move it to the vault."

The team sprang into action, their movements frantic but coordinated. Years of research, countless experiments, critical data—it was all stored within the walls of this base, and losing it would mean losing everything. Martinez couldn't let that happen. They were too close to a breakthrough, too close to understanding the tree's core.

Another rumble shook the base, this one stronger than the last. Martinez stumbled, gripping the edge of the table to steady herself. She could hear the distant sound of gunfire, the muffled shouts of security personnel trying to hold the line. The aberrations were already inside the outer perimeter.

"David," Martinez called, her voice strained. "Get the backup drives. I'll secure the physical data."

Johansson nodded, sprinting toward the far side of the lab, where the team kept their backup servers. Martinez turned to the shelves stacked with binders and folders, her hands trembling as she began gathering the most crucial documents. The sound of chaos grew louder—the aberrations were closing in.

As she reached for a stack of papers, the lights flickered, and the ground shook violently. The walls groaned as if the earth itself was tearing apart. A deafening crash echoed through the facility, followed by the unmistakable sound of metal being torn apart.

"They're inside!" someone shouted from the corridor.

Martinez's heart pounded in her chest as she clutched the papers to her chest. The door to the lab burst open, and several members of the security team rushed inside, their weapons raised.

"We have to move, now!" one of the guards yelled, his voice filled with urgency. "The aberrations are breaching the inner sections. We can't hold them off much longer."

Martinez hesitated for only a moment, her eyes darting to the monitors still displaying critical data. Years of work. It couldn't end like this.

Another explosion rocked the base, and the ceiling cracked, sending dust and debris raining down. The guards grabbed Martinez by the arm, pulling her toward the exit.

"Dr. Martinez, we have to go!"

She stumbled after them, barely able to keep her footing as the base continued to shake. The sound of gunfire and monstrous roars filled the air, the walls vibrating with the sheer force of the attack. Johansson appeared beside her, carrying a small box of drives, his face pale and stricken.

"We've lost half the data," he gasped, his voice tight with panic. "The backup servers were hit. I got what I could."

Martinez felt her chest tighten. Half the data. Half of everything they had worked for. The thought made her stomach churn, but there was no time to process the loss. They needed to get out before the base collapsed entirely.

As they made their way through the corridors, the devastation became clearer. The walls were cracked and splintered, sections of the base caving in as the aberrations tore through it like a wave of destruction. Bodies littered the floor—security personnel, researchers, people Martinez had known for years, all fallen in the onslaught.

Her mind raced, desperate to make sense of what was happening, but the reality was clear. They had underestimated the aberrations. The creatures had evolved, becoming more coordinated, more dangerous. They had learned how to breach the base's defenses, and now there was nothing standing in their way.

When they reached the final hallway leading to the exit, the sight that greeted them made Martinez's blood run cold. The aberrations had broken through. Their twisted, grotesque forms writhed in the distance, tearing through the walls with unnatural speed. The guards opened fire, but the creatures were relentless, their bodies absorbing the bullets as they surged forward.

"We're not going to make it," Johansson muttered, his voice filled with despair.

"Keep moving!" Martinez shouted, pushing him forward. "We have to make it!"

The group sprinted toward the exit, the sound of the aberrations closing in behind them like a tidal wave of horror. Martinez's heart raced as they reached the reinforced doors that led to the surface. They were so close. So close to escaping.

But as they reached the doors, the ground shook again, and a massive crash echoed through the base. Martinez turned, her eyes widening in horror as she saw the ceiling begin to cave in. A section of the wall collapsed, and the aberrations poured through the breach, their eyes glowing with a sickly, predatory light.

"Go!" Martinez screamed, shoving Johansson toward the door.

The guards fired their weapons, trying to hold the creatures back, but it was no use. The aberrations moved with terrifying speed, tearing through the guards like paper. Martinez barely had time to process what was happening before she felt the ground beneath her give way. She hit the floor hard, the impact knocking the wind from her lungs.

For a moment, everything was a blur—dust, debris, the deafening roar of the aberrations closing in. And then, through the chaos, she saw it: her lab, her work, the years of research they had fought so hard to preserve, being torn apart.

The monitors flickered one last time before turning off. The sound of glass breaking and the screams of her team echoed through the hallways. Dr. Martinez fell to her knees in front of what remained of her notes.

Everything—years of work, years of struggle—was disappearing in a whirlwind of chaos and destruction.

Her hands shook as she reached for the scattered papers, the binders that had been torn from the shelves, but it was no use. It was gone. Everything was gone.

"We have to go, now!" Johansson yelled, pulling her to her feet. "Isabel, we have to go!"

Martinez blinked, the world spinning around her. She looked at the shattered remnants of her work, the scattered fragments of the research they had sacrificed so much for, and felt a crushing weight settle over her chest.

It was over.

With one final glance at the destruction, Martinez let Johansson pull her toward the exit. The few remaining survivors stumbled through the doors and into the night, the cold air hitting them like a slap in the face. Behind them, the base collapsed in on itself, swallowed by the chaos.

Martinez stood in the open air, her heart pounding, her mind numb with shock. The base was gone. The research was gone.

And with it, their last hope.

CHAPTER 22
Preparing for War

Isaac hadn't realized how quiet the world had become until the low, unsettling hum of the **Inquisition's headquarters** filled his ears. The ancient underground facility was hidden beneath the ruins of what had once been a bustling city, and now served as a fortress of last hope. The atmosphere inside was tense, charged with the weight of impending conflict, but it was a different kind of tension from the one Isaac had grown used to during his isolation. This was a place where people were focused on one thing: war.

He had been brought here by **Lydia** and **Vernon**, the Inquisitors who had first approached him weeks ago, offering him a path forward. Isaac had hesitated then, uncertain about the secretive organization's methods and their shadowy history. But after the Inquisition had revealed the tree's ancient origins—and after witnessing the devastation spreading around him—he had realized he had no choice. Whatever misgivings he had about the Inquisition, they were the only ones with a plan. And now, that plan was coming together.

Isaac moved through the winding halls of the headquarters, past rooms filled with old, forbidden technology and strange artifacts that glowed faintly in the dim light. Sorcerers and scientists alike were at work, their heads bent over diagrams and ancient texts, their hands covered in soot and ash from experiments that defied the natural order. Isaac couldn't help but feel out of place, a small cog in a machine he barely understood.

But he had a role to play. Lydia had told him as much. The tree in his yard, one of the largest and most dangerous, had somehow failed to fully consume him. He had survived its influence longer than anyone else they had found, and that made him valuable to their mission. He was to be a key player in the final assault on the tree.

As he approached the war room, Isaac paused, feeling a surge of anxiety rise in his chest. Inside, leaders from the **Underground Resistance**, the **Inquisition**, and what remained of the **Global Research Initiative on Anomalous Phenomena (GRIAP)** were gathered, laying the groundwork for what they all knew would be their last stand. Isaac took a deep breath and stepped inside.

Tensions Between Allies

The room was a chaotic mixture of high-tech equipment and ancient tools of sorcery. Large monitors displayed maps of the world, overlaid with the spreading influence of the trees, while strange symbols and artifacts lay scattered across the tables. At the head of the room stood Lydia, her sharp eyes scanning the assembled group, while Vernon stood stoically beside her, his arms crossed over his chest.

On the opposite side of the room, **Kellar**, the embittered leader of the Underground Resistance, paced back and forth, his movements tense and angry. Behind him, the few survivors of the resistance stood, their faces hard, their bodies battered from months of fighting. Kellar had never fully trusted the Inquisition, and that distrust was clear now more than ever.

"We've been fighting these things for months," Kellar snapped, his voice filled with frustration. "And now you expect us to just fall in line and follow your plan? A plan that's based on what—sorcery? Magic?"

Lydia's gaze remained steady, unflinching. "It's not just sorcery, Kellar. Our plan is based on centuries of knowledge. The trees are not a simple enemy. They are a force tied to the very fabric of this world's reality. You've seen what they can do, haven't you? They defy logic, break the laws of physics. Your conventional weapons can't stop them."

Kellar's eyes narrowed. "We've taken down nests before. We've killed aberrations. Don't tell me we can't fight."

"You've fought bravely," Vernon interjected, his voice low and measured. "But the trees are evolving. They're adapting to every tactic you've used against them. Your last mission—it cost you most of your people. If you go out there again, unprepared, the same thing will happen."

Isaac stood at the edge of the room, watching the tension rise between the two groups. The resistance fighters were hardened, their faces lined with anger and grief, but he could see the cracks forming. They had suffered too many losses. Kellar's bitterness ran deep, but it was clear that even he knew they couldn't keep fighting like this.

Across the room, **Dr. Isabel Martinez** sat hunched over a table, sifting through the salvaged data her team had managed to rescue from the destroyed research base. Her face was pale and drawn, her eyes shadowed by exhaustion, but her hands moved with purpose. The research group had lost almost everything in the attack, but they had preserved enough to make a difference. Enough to help the Inquisition's plan.

"We've confirmed that the roots are the key," Martinez said, her voice cutting through the tension. All eyes turned toward her as she continued. "The tree's roots are connected to the distortions we've been seeing—gravity, time, even reality itself. If we can sever the connection between the tree and its roots, we might be able to stop it."

Lydia nodded, stepping forward to address the group. "The trees are feeding off something deeper, something older than we can fully understand. The roots are their lifeline. Destroying the tree itself won't work unless we take out the roots, the very core of their power."

"But how do we get close enough?" one of Kellar's lieutenants asked, his voice tense. "The aberrations will tear us apart before we can even touch the roots."

Isaac felt his stomach knot at the question. The trees had created an impenetrable fortress around themselves, a nightmare landscape filled with aberrations and twisting realities. Getting to the roots, getting close enough to do any real damage, seemed impossible. But they didn't have a choice. They had to try.

Lydia turned her gaze to Isaac, her eyes narrowing slightly as if she could see the fear running through him. "That's where Isaac comes in."

Everyone in the room turned to look at him, and Isaac felt a wave of pressure settle over him. He wasn't a soldier. He wasn't a scientist or a strategist. But he had survived the tree's influence longer than anyone. And for reasons he couldn't fully understand, the Inquisition believed he could get close enough to the roots to make a difference.

"The tree in Isaac's yard is one of the oldest, one of the strongest," Lydia explained. "Yet, for reasons we're still studying, Isaac has been able to withstand its influence. He has lived near the tree for longer than anyone else we've encountered, and he remains... functional."

Isaac winced at the word. **Functional**. That's all he was now—a tool to be used in their desperate plan. But he knew it was true. He had survived longer than most, and if that meant he had to be the one to get close to the tree's core, then so be it.

Kellar crossed his arms, his expression skeptical. "You're saying he's immune? That doesn't make him invincible. The aberrations will still come for him, just like they've come for everyone else."

"He's not immune," Vernon said, his voice calm. "But there's something about his connection to the tree that we need to exploit. We believe that Isaac can get close enough to plant the charges we need to sever the roots."

Isaac's breath caught in his throat. **Plant the charges?** He had known he would play a role, but this... this was far more than he had expected. They were putting everything on him.

Lydia stepped forward, her gaze softening slightly as she addressed him directly. "I know this is a lot to ask, Isaac. But you've survived this long for a reason. The tree chose you. You've resisted its influence. We believe you can get close enough to do what no one else can."

Isaac swallowed hard, his mind racing. He didn't know if he was ready for this. But what choice did he have? The world was crumbling, and if they didn't stop the tree now, there wouldn't be anything left to save.

He took a deep breath, steadying himself before nodding. "I'll do it."

Kellar's eyes flickered with doubt, but he said nothing. The resistance leader was used to doing things his way, relying on brute force and sheer will to fight the aberrations. But even he knew that their old methods wouldn't work here.

Martinez stood up from her place at the table, holding a small device in her hand. "We've developed charges specifically designed to destabilize the tree's roots. They'll need to be placed in several key locations, deep beneath the tree's core. It won't be easy, but if Isaac can get close enough, we might be able to sever the tree's connection to reality."

Isaac stared at the device, his mind buzzing with the weight of what he was being asked to do. It all came down to this—getting close enough to plant the charges, close enough to strike at the very heart of the tree. If he failed, the consequences would be catastrophic. But if he succeeded...

"We'll provide support," Vernon said, his voice firm. "Kellar's team will cover the perimeter, taking down as many aberrations as possible while Isaac moves in. The Inquisition will provide additional support with our own forces."

Kellar's jaw tightened, but he nodded reluctantly. "Fine. But if this goes wrong, I'm not taking the blame."

Lydia ignored his comment, her eyes fixed on Isaac. "We all know the risks. But this is our best chance. Isaac, we'll be with you every step of the way."

Isaac nodded again, feeling the weight of the world on his shoulders. The plan was set. The final assault was coming.

And there was no turning back.

CHAPTER 23

The First Assault

Isaac's heart raced as he stood with the rest of the assault team at the edge of the tree's vast, corrupted perimeter. The landscape ahead was a twisted nightmare, a stark contrast to the once-familiar streets and homes that had surrounded the tree months ago. Now, the ground itself seemed to pulse with a dark energy, warped roots slithering through the cracked earth, and the air hung heavy with an oppressive stillness that gnawed at the mind.

The assault team, a grim mix of **Inquisition soldiers, Underground Resistance fighters**, and a handful of survivors from various outposts, had gathered here with one goal: to strike at the heart of the tree. Isaac felt the weight of his task pressing down on him—he was the one who would have to get close enough to plant the charges beneath the roots. He was the one who would have to venture deeper into the nightmare than anyone else.

The voices around him were tense, filled with both hope and doubt. No one knew what to expect once they made their move. The aberrations that protected the tree had grown more vicious, more intelligent, and no one had ever gotten close enough to touch the roots without being torn apart.

Isaac glanced at **Lydia** and **Vernon**, who were overseeing the operation from behind the front lines. Lydia caught his eye and gave him a steady nod, as if to remind him of the importance of his role. Kellar stood a little further ahead, his body tense, his expression unreadable as he barked orders to his remaining fighters. The last mission had nearly broken him, but Kellar's bitterness had only hardened his resolve. He would die before retreating again.

The plan was simple, at least in theory. The Inquisition and the Resistance would work together to clear a path through the aberrations, distracting the creatures long enough for Isaac to reach the tree's roots and plant the charges. But Isaac could feel the uncertainty hanging over the group like a thick fog. They had never faced anything on this scale before, and the tree's defenses were far more advanced than they had anticipated.

Vernon's voice crackled over the comms. "Prepare to move. The aberrations will be on us the moment we make contact. Stick to the plan and stay sharp."

Isaac checked his gear one last time, his hands trembling slightly as he adjusted the small pack of explosives strapped to his back. The charges were compact but powerful—specially designed by the remnants of the Research Group to destabilize the tree's root system. He just needed to get close enough to plant them.

"Remember," Lydia said, her voice calm but firm, "we only get one shot at this. If we fail here, there won't be another chance. We press forward, no matter what."

Isaac nodded, steeling himself for what was to come. There was no turning back now.

The Assault Begins

The first strike came with a thunderous roar. Kellar's team moved in first, launching a barrage of explosives toward the nearest aberration nests. The ground shook as the blasts ripped through the air, sending debris flying. The aberrations reacted immediately, their twisted, monstrous forms surging out from the shadows, their glowing eyes locking onto the approaching fighters with terrifying intensity.

Isaac followed closely behind the first wave of soldiers, his heart pounding in his chest as he watched the chaos unfold. The aberrations moved with unnatural speed, their limbs contorting as they charged toward the attackers. Gunfire erupted all around him, the sharp crack of bullets cutting through the eerie stillness. But no matter how many aberrations were cut down, more seemed to pour from the shadows, their numbers seemingly endless.

Kellar's voice boomed over the comms. "Focus on the nests! We need to clear the path for Isaac!"

Isaac ducked behind a crumbling wall as an aberration lunged toward him, its clawed hand swiping through the air where he had been standing moments before. He could feel the heat of the creature's breath as it snarled, its eyes burning with malice. Before it could strike again, one of Kellar's fighters opened fire, the bullets tearing through the aberration's grotesque body and sending it crashing to the ground.

"Move, Isaac!" the fighter yelled, motioning him forward.

Isaac scrambled to his feet and sprinted toward the tree's base, the ground beneath him shifting and pulsing with the same unnatural energy he had come to know so well. The tree loomed above him, its gnarled branches twisting up into the blood-red sky, casting long shadows that seemed to flicker and writhe like living things. Every step he took felt heavier, as if the tree was actively resisting his approach.

The aberrations kept coming, their numbers growing as the Inquisition and Resistance fighters tried to hold the line. Isaac could hear the shouts of his comrades, the crackle of gunfire, and the deafening roar of explosives, but it all seemed distant now, muted by the overwhelming presence of the tree. It was as if the tree itself was alive, watching him, waiting for him to make a mistake.

Suddenly, the ground beneath Isaac's feet trembled violently, and he stumbled, barely managing to catch himself before falling. He looked up, his breath catching in his throat. The tree had begun to move.

Its roots, massive and dark, twisted and writhed beneath the surface, tearing through the earth with a slow, deliberate motion. The tree was reacting to their assault, its very core shifting and adjusting as if it could sense the danger approaching. Isaac's mind raced as he realized what was happening: the tree was adapting. It was defending itself in ways they hadn't anticipated.

"We're losing control!" Kellar's voice crackled through the comms, filled with panic. "The aberrations are—"

A deafening explosion cut off his words, and Isaac felt the ground shake violently beneath him. One of the nests had erupted in flames, sending a shockwave through the battlefield. The force of the blast knocked Isaac off his feet, and he hit the ground hard, his vision blurring as pain shot through his body.

For a moment, everything went silent. Isaac lay on the ground, dazed, the world spinning around him. He could hear the distant sound of gunfire, the shouts of the soldiers, but it all felt far away, as if he were drifting through a dream. Slowly, painfully, he pushed himself to his knees, trying to regain his bearings.

And that's when he saw it.

The tree was regenerating.

The roots that had been damaged by the explosives were already knitting themselves back together, the bark sealing over the wounds as if nothing had happened. The tree was healing faster than they could damage it. Every strike they made was undone in moments.

Isaac's heart sank. They weren't ready for this. The tree was too powerful, too adaptive. If they couldn't destroy the roots, if the charges weren't enough, then everything would be for nothing.

His mind raced as he tried to think of a way forward. They couldn't retreat—there was no going back. But how could they stop something that could regenerate this quickly?

It was then that Isaac remembered the **Vagabond's Diary**. During one of the quieter moments before the assault, Isaac had found another entry, scrawled in the margins of the journal. It had been brief, almost hurried, but the words had stayed with him:

Vagabond's Diary - Forgotten Entry

"We tried before. Years ago, before anyone knew what the trees really were. We thought fire would stop it. We thought bombs could destroy it. But it heals. It always heals. Every time we cut it down, it grows back stronger. The roots go too deep. Too deep for any of us to reach."

"There is no end. The tree doesn't die. It regenerates, faster every time. We thought we had won, but the moment we turned away, it was back. The same tree, the same nightmare. It never ends."

Isaac had brushed off the entry at the time, assuming the writer's despair had colored their perception. But now, staring at the regenerating roots, he understood. The tree's ability to heal wasn't just a defense—it was a weapon. Every failure made it stronger. Every attempt to destroy it only fed its power.

"We're not ready for this," Isaac muttered, his voice barely audible over the chaos around him.

The realization hit him like a punch to the gut. This wasn't just a physical battle—they were fighting something far more complex, something that operated on levels they didn't fully understand. The tree wasn't just a living organism—it was an anomaly, something that twisted the very fabric of reality. And they were woefully unprepared.

Isaac clenched his fists, a surge of frustration rising in his chest. But there was no time to dwell on their mistakes. The aberrations were still coming, and the tree was still growing. If they didn't press on, they would be overwhelmed. They had no choice but to move forward.

He pushed himself to his feet, his body aching from the fall, and forced himself to keep moving. The charges were still in his pack, and as long as there was a chance, he had to try. They weren't ready—but they had to press on.

There was no turning back.

CHAPTER 24
Fragmented Hope

The camp was a somber wreckage of battered souls and broken bodies. The weight of failure hung heavy in the air as Isaac wandered through the makeshift medical tents, seeing the haunted faces of survivors—what few remained. The **first assault** on the tree had been a disaster. What was supposed to be their moment of triumph had turned into a massacre. The aberrations had torn through their ranks, and the tree's defenses had proven stronger than anyone had imagined.

Isaac's heart weighed heavy in his chest as he walked past rows of injured fighters, some groaning in pain, others lying eerily still, their minds lost to the nightmares the tree had inflicted on them. He hadn't escaped unscathed either; bruises, burns, and cuts marred his skin, but the physical wounds were nothing compared to the emotional toll. The loss of life—the sheer devastation—was impossible to shake.

He sat down on the edge of a collapsed wall, staring at the distant silhouette of the tree, its enormous, twisted branches blotting out the crimson sky. Every time he looked at it, the tree seemed bigger, more malevolent, as if it had fed off the violence and chaos of the battle. Its roots twisted into the ground like claws, digging deeper into the earth, spreading corruption with every inch they grew.

"We weren't ready for this," Isaac muttered to himself, his hands shaking. "We'll never be ready."

The sound of footsteps behind him pulled him from his thoughts. **Dr. Isabel Martinez**, looking pale and worn, approached him slowly. Her face was gaunt from sleepless nights, her eyes hollowed by grief and exhaustion. In her hands was a tablet, and Isaac could see that it was filled with data—numbers, graphs, and maps of the tree's growth and influence.

"It's worse than we thought," she said quietly, sitting down beside him.

Isaac glanced at the tablet, his stomach turning. "What do you mean?"

Martinez sighed, rubbing her temples as if she could physically force the tension from her body. "The tree is growing faster. The data shows that after each assault, it regenerates, but it doesn't just heal—it evolves. The more we hurt it, the more it adapts."

Isaac's heart sank. "So, everything we're doing is making it stronger?"

Martinez shook her head. "Not stronger, exactly—just harder to kill. It learns from us, from every attack. It's like it's anticipating our moves before we even make them."

Isaac clenched his fists, frustration boiling beneath his skin. "So what are we supposed to do? We can't just keep throwing ourselves at it. We'll all die before we even make a dent."

"We've found something," Martinez said, her voice barely above a whisper. "It's not much, but it's something."

Isaac turned to look at her, his brow furrowed. "What do you mean?"

Martinez handed him the tablet, her fingers trembling slightly as she did. "We've been working day and night, even as the base collapsed around us. We've lost people—good people. But we managed to compile enough data before the aberrations hit us. It's not perfect, but it might be the key."

Isaac scrolled through the information, his eyes scanning the screen. The data showed the intricate network of the tree's roots, their spread through the earth like a web of corruption. But what caught his attention was a small, glowing marker at the heart of the tree's root system—a **core**, pulsating like a heartbeat.

"The core," he murmured, remembering the passage from the **Vagabond's Diary**. "The tree feeds off this. This is what's keeping it alive."

Martinez nodded. "We think so. The core is buried deep beneath the tree's roots. It's protected by layers of defenses—aberrations, gravitational distortions, time warps—but if we can destroy it…"

"We can destroy the tree," Isaac finished, hope flickering in his chest.

"It won't be easy," Martinez warned, her voice grave. "The tree has evolved to protect its core. We've already lost people trying to get close enough to study it. But we think that with the right tools, the right strategy, we might have a chance."

Isaac stared at the glowing marker on the screen, feeling the weight of her words sink in. The **first assault** had been brutal, and they had lost so much. But this… this was a glimmer of hope. A fragile, flickering light in the darkness.

"How many more lives?" Isaac asked, his voice cracking with emotion. "How many more people do we lose before we end this?"

Martinez's eyes darkened, her expression pained. "I don't know. But if we don't try, we'll lose everything. The tree is spreading. Cities are falling. The aberrations are getting stronger. If we don't stop it soon, there won't be anyone left to fight."

Isaac's mind raced. The data in front of him was their best chance, but the thought of sending more people into the fray, knowing how many had already died, made his stomach turn. He thought of **Kellar**, the leader of the Underground Resistance, and the few remaining fighters who were still willing to fight, despite everything they had lost. They were barely holding it together. Morale was low, and the tension between the Resistance and the Inquisition was growing worse by the day.

"How do we even get close to it?" Isaac asked, his voice filled with doubt. "We couldn't even reach the roots last time."

"We'll need to coordinate everything perfectly," Martinez said, determination creeping into her voice. "The Resistance can draw the aberrations away, keep them distracted while we move in. The Inquisition has tools—ancient tech that can disrupt the tree's defenses, at least temporarily. But it'll cost us."

Isaac knew what she meant. Every time they made a move, people died. Every strike, every skirmish, came at the cost of lives—good people, brave people who believed in the fight but were swallowed by the tree's influence before they even got close.

"I'll go," Isaac said suddenly, his voice steady despite the fear gnawing at him. "If this is our best shot, I'll do it."

Martinez blinked, her tired eyes widening slightly. "Isaac, you've already—"

"I've already survived this long," he interrupted, his jaw clenched. "I've survived the tree's influence. I've stayed close to it longer than anyone else, and I'm still standing. If anyone has a chance of getting close to that core, it's me."

Martinez looked at him for a long moment, her expression unreadable. Then she nodded, a sad smile playing on her lips. "You might be right."

Before Isaac could respond, the sound of an argument echoed across the camp. He and Martinez both turned to see **Kellar** and **Lydia** in a heated discussion near the edge of the medical tents. The Resistance leader's face was red with anger, his hands gesturing wildly as he spoke.

"We can't just keep sending people in to die!" Kellar shouted, his voice filled with fury. "We've already lost too many. How many more of my people are you going to sacrifice for this insane plan?"

Lydia's expression was calm, but there was a hardness in her eyes. "This isn't just about your people, Kellar. This is about the world. If we don't stop the tree, everyone dies. We need your help, whether you like it or not."

Kellar clenched his fists, his eyes burning with frustration. "We've been fighting these things for months. You show up with your ancient magic and your promises, but all we've seen is death. How can we trust you?"

"You don't have to trust me," Lydia replied coldly. "But you do have to decide if you're willing to fight."

The tension between them was palpable, the air thick with the weight of their argument. Isaac stood up, ready to intervene, but before he could, Martinez placed a hand on his arm.

"Let them argue," she said quietly. "It's all they have left."

Isaac watched as Kellar stormed away, his anger radiating off him like a palpable force. The Resistance was falling apart, their numbers dwindling with every failed mission. And yet, they were still willing to fight. Still willing to risk everything for a chance at stopping the tree.

"We're all falling apart," Isaac muttered, his voice heavy with despair. "How do we keep going?"

Martinez looked at him, her eyes filled with a quiet sadness. "We don't have a choice. We keep going because if we don't… there's nothing left."

Isaac nodded, though the weight of her words pressed down on him like a stone. They were running out of time, out of lives, out of hope. But the data in his hands—the core at the heart of the tree—it was something. It was a chance, no matter how small.

And right now, a chance was all they had left.

CHAPTER 25
Beginning the Assault

The sky above the battlefield was a deep, unnatural crimson, a constant reminder of the tree's corrupting presence. The air smelled of charred earth and decay, thick with the oppressive hum of the tree's influence as it spread through the ground beneath their feet. Isaac stood at the forefront, the weight of responsibility heavy on his shoulders. This was it—the moment they had been building toward. The **final assault** was about to begin, and Isaac knew that whether they succeeded or failed, this would be their last stand.

Around him, the remnants of the **Underground Resistance**, soldiers from the **Inquisition**, and a handful of sorcerers from the Inquisition's secretive order gathered, their faces grim but resolute. There was no room for doubt anymore. They had all seen too much death, too much horror, to turn back now. The tree loomed in the distance, its massive, twisted branches stretching impossibly high into the sky, blotting out the fading light. The core—buried deep beneath the earth, protected by layers of the tree's roots and the swarms of aberrations—was their target. If they could reach it, destroy it, then maybe—just maybe—they could stop this nightmare once and for all.

Isaac glanced around at the gathered forces, feeling the tension thick in the air. **Kellar** stood nearby, his face a hardened mask of determination. Despite the losses and the bitter grudges, Kellar and the remaining members of the Resistance were ready to fight. They had no illusions left—most of them didn't expect to survive this, but they would give their lives to stop the tree. Next to Kellar, **Lydia** and **Vernon** were deep in conversation with the sorcerers, discussing the final preparations for the assault. The Inquisition's secret weapons—ancient technologies fused with forbidden sorcery—would be their edge in this battle, though none of them fully understood how or why the tree would respond to these tools.

Dr. Isabel Martinez stood a short distance away, her eyes focused on a holographic map of the tree's root system projected from her tablet. The data they had collected—paid for with the lives of her research team—was now the foundation of their strategy. The map showed the locations of the tree's key roots, the ones feeding directly into the core. Those would be the targets, the places where Isaac and the others would plant the charges and strike the killing blow.

Isaac swallowed hard, trying to push down the rising tide of fear. He wasn't a soldier. He wasn't a leader. But here he was, about to lead an army of desperate fighters into what could very well be their final moments. The hum of the tree echoed in his mind, a constant reminder of its power, its malevolent will pressing against him. It felt like the tree was watching them, knowing they were coming, waiting for them to make their move.

"It's time," Lydia said, her voice cutting through the silence as she approached Isaac. She nodded toward the gathered forces, the last remnants of humanity's resistance. "Everything's ready. We move as soon as you give the word."

Isaac nodded, feeling a lump form in his throat. His mind flashed back to all the moments that had led to this—the discovery of the seed, the emergence of the tree, the first horrifying encounter with the aberrations. He hadn't asked for any of this, but somehow, he had been thrust into the center of it all. Now, it was time to finish what had started.

"Alright," he said, his voice steady despite the fear gnawing at him. "Let's get this done."

The March Toward the Tree

The group began their advance, moving slowly through the twisted, warped landscape that surrounded the tree. The ground was uneven, cracked and broken by the tree's roots, which pulsed beneath the surface like veins of a living organism. The air was thick with the smell of rot, and the low hum of the tree's influence seemed to vibrate through the earth, making every step feel heavier than it should.

Isaac led the way, his heart pounding in his chest. Behind him, the soldiers of the Inquisition moved with precision, their weapons at the ready. The Resistance fighters, hardened by months of battle, followed closely, their eyes scanning the horizon for any sign of the aberrations. They knew the creatures would be waiting for them, lurking in the shadows, ready to strike at the first opportunity.

Lydia and the sorcerers remained near the center of the group, their hands glowing faintly with the energy of the ancient spells they were preparing to unleash. Isaac had seen the power of the Inquisition's sorcery before, during the first assault, and he knew they would need every bit of it to survive what was coming. The aberrations weren't just mindless monsters anymore—they had grown stronger, more coordinated, as the tree fed on their fear and destruction.

As they drew closer to the tree, the ground began to shift beneath their feet, the gravitational distortions becoming more pronounced. Time itself seemed to warp around them—moments stretched and snapped back unpredictably, making it difficult to tell how far they had traveled or how much time had passed. Isaac's mind buzzed with the sensation, but he forced himself to focus. The tree was trying to disorient them, but they couldn't afford to lose their way now.

"Stay close!" Kellar barked, his voice sharp. "Keep your eyes on the target!"

Isaac glanced over at Kellar, who was scanning the landscape with a practiced eye. Despite their differences, Isaac respected the man's tenacity. Kellar had lost more than most, but he kept fighting. Even now, as the odds stacked against them, he refused to give in to despair.

Suddenly, a ripple of movement caught Isaac's attention. He froze, raising a hand to signal the others. The group halted, their weapons at the ready, as Isaac squinted into the distance.

"There," Lydia whispered, her eyes narrowing. "They're coming."

Out of the shadows, the **aberrations** emerged—twisted, nightmarish creatures with too many eyes and limbs that moved in unnatural, jerky motions. Their bodies seemed to flicker in and out of focus, as if they were caught between two planes of existence, and their hollow, glowing eyes fixed on the group with a malevolent hunger.

"They know we're here," Vernon muttered, stepping forward, his weapon raised. "Get ready."

The Battle Begins

The air seemed to crackle with tension as the aberrations closed in. They moved faster than Isaac remembered, their grotesque forms darting across the broken landscape with a terrifying speed. The first wave hit hard, slamming into the front lines of the Inquisition soldiers, their claws slicing through armor and flesh.

"Open fire!" Kellar roared, and the air was filled with the sound of gunfire and the hum of energy weapons as the soldiers unleashed everything they had. Bullets tore through the aberrations, but for every one that fell, two more seemed to take its place. The creatures were relentless, their bodies writhing and contorting as they charged forward.

Isaac's heart raced as he raised his own weapon, firing into the mass of creatures. Around him, the sorcerers unleashed their spells—bolts of energy and arcs of light that tore through the air, striking the aberrations with explosive force. The ground trembled as the battle raged, and the smell of ozone filled Isaac's nostrils as the sorcery clashed with the tree's influence.

"We need to move!" Lydia shouted over the chaos. "If we stay here, they'll overwhelm us!"

Isaac nodded, his eyes scanning the battlefield for a way through. The aberrations were everywhere, but they couldn't afford to be bogged down. Their goal was the tree's core—if they didn't reach it soon, the tree would regenerate, and everything they had fought for would be lost.

"Follow me!" Isaac shouted, pushing through the thick of the battle, cutting down an aberration that lunged at him with its spiked limbs. "We can't let them pin us down!"

The group rallied around him, cutting a path through the swarm of aberrations. The sorcerers provided cover, their spells forming barriers of light that kept the creatures at bay, but it wouldn't last long. The aberrations were relentless, their numbers seemingly endless.

Isaac's mind raced as they pressed forward, the tree looming closer with every step. The ground beneath them shifted and twisted, gravity pulling them in strange directions as they neared the heart of the tree's influence. Time felt like it was slipping away, stretching out and collapsing in on itself as the battle raged.

But despite the chaos, Isaac felt a strange sense of clarity. This was it. The final push. They had no choice but to keep going, no matter the cost.

And then, through the smoke and fire, Isaac saw it—the entrance to the **tree's core**. A massive, gnarled opening in the ground, surrounded by twisted roots and pulsing with a dark, malevolent energy.

"We're almost there!" he shouted, his voice hoarse. "Keep moving!"

As the group surged forward, Isaac couldn't shake the feeling that something was watching them—something far more dangerous than the aberrations they had been fighting. The tree was waiting for them, and whatever lay at its heart would not go down without a fight.

The battle was far from over.

CHAPTER 26

Kellar's Death

The ground trembled beneath Isaac's feet as the battle raged on, the air thick with the acrid smell of smoke and blood. The twisted aberrations were relentless, pouring forth from the shadows like a swarm of nightmares, their many-eyed forms darting through the chaotic battlefield. Isaac could barely hear anything over the cacophony of gunfire, the hum of sorcery, and the grotesque screeches of the aberrations as they fell or regenerated, their bodies writhing in unnatural ways.

He pushed forward, leading the group closer to the tree's core, the entrance looming just ahead like the maw of some ancient, malevolent beast. But every step forward came at a cost—lives were being lost. The Inquisition soldiers and Resistance fighters were holding the line, but for how much longer? Isaac could see the strain in their faces, the exhaustion in their movements.

And then there was **Kellar**.

Kellar fought with the ferocity of a man who had nothing left to lose. His eyes burned with a mixture of hatred and desperation, his movements sharp and brutal as he cut down one aberration after another. He had always been the backbone of the **Underground Resistance**, the one who had kept them fighting even when hope seemed distant. But now, as the battle reached its climax, Isaac could see that Kellar's rage was driving him toward something dangerous. The man was consumed, his hatred for the aberrations and the tree pushing him beyond the limits of his body and mind.

"Fall back!" Isaac shouted over the chaos, his voice barely carrying above the noise. "We need to regroup!"

But Kellar didn't listen. He was too far gone, too deep in his own need for vengeance. Isaac watched as Kellar charged forward, his face contorted with fury, cutting a path through the aberrations with brutal efficiency. His strikes were powerful but reckless, each blow delivered with the force of a man who no longer cared if he lived or died.

"Kellar!" Isaac screamed, trying to catch his attention. But the Resistance leader didn't look back.

Isaac gritted his teeth, turning to Lydia, who was fending off an aberration with a blast of light. "We have to stop him! He's going to get himself killed!"

Lydia's eyes followed Isaac's gaze, and a flash of understanding crossed her face. She nodded grimly, but there was little they could do. The battlefield was too chaotic, and Kellar was too far ahead, already lost in his own rage.

Kellar was pushing toward the heart of the tree's defenses, where the aberrations were thickest. His movements were frantic, his breath ragged, but there was a singular focus in his eyes: the destruction of the tree. The hatred he carried, the bitterness that had driven him this far, had finally taken control. He wanted nothing more than to bring the whole thing crashing down, no matter the cost.

Isaac watched helplessly as Kellar cut down another aberration, his blade slicing through the creature's grotesque form. But for every one that fell, another took its place, and Isaac could see that Kellar was starting to falter. His attacks grew sloppier, his movements slower, and the swarm of aberrations began to close in around him.

"Kellar!" Isaac shouted again, his voice breaking with desperation.

But it was too late.

The aberrations swarmed Kellar, their many-eyed forms circling him like vultures. He fought them off as best he could, his blade flashing in the dim light, but he was outnumbered. One aberration lunged at him, its spiked limbs catching him across the chest, tearing through his armor. Kellar stumbled, blood pouring from the wound, but he didn't stop. He swung wildly, cutting the creature down, but another took its place, and then another.

Isaac's heart pounded in his chest as he watched Kellar go down, the aberrations piling on top of him, tearing at his body with claws and teeth. Kellar screamed, a sound filled with both rage and pain, but he didn't stop fighting. Even as his body failed him, even as the aberrations tore him apart, he kept swinging, kept fighting.

And then, in a final act of defiance, Kellar pulled a small device from his belt—one of the charges they had prepared to destroy the tree's core. His bloodied fingers fumbled with it for a moment, but then he activated it, a grim smile crossing his face as he looked up at the tree.

"For all of them," Kellar muttered, his voice barely a whisper.

The explosion was sudden and violent, a blast of energy that sent shockwaves through the battlefield. The aberrations surrounding Kellar were blown apart, their bodies disintegrating in the blast. The force of the explosion sent Isaac and the others stumbling back, the ground shaking beneath them as debris flew through the air.

When the dust settled, there was nothing left of Kellar but a scorched patch of earth, surrounded by the remains of the aberrations he had destroyed in his final moments.

Isaac stared at the spot where Kellar had fallen, his heart heavy with grief and anger. Kellar had been a difficult man, driven by bitterness and hatred, but he had been their leader. He had kept the Resistance alive when no one else could. And now, he was gone—sacrificed in a desperate attempt to buy them time.

Lydia approached Isaac, her face pale but determined. "He bought us a chance," she said quietly. "We need to take it."

Isaac nodded, though his throat felt tight with emotion. Kellar's death had not been in vain. The explosion had cleared a path through the aberrations, giving them a brief window to press forward. But the cost was high, and the weight of Kellar's sacrifice hung over them like a shroud.

Pushing Forward

The survivors of the Resistance and the Inquisition regrouped quickly, their faces grim but resolute. Kellar's death had shaken them, but it had also given them a spark of renewed purpose. They had lost so much already, but they couldn't afford to lose focus now. The tree's core was within reach, and they couldn't let Kellar's sacrifice go to waste.

Isaac led the way, his heart pounding in his chest as they pushed deeper into the heart of the tree's defenses. The ground beneath them was slick with the blood of the fallen, both human and aberration alike. The air was thick with the scent of smoke and death, but there was no time to grieve, no time to hesitate.

Around them, the aberrations continued to swarm, but the explosion had weakened their ranks. The soldiers and sorcerers of the Inquisition fought with a renewed fury, cutting down the creatures with every ounce of strength they had left. The path ahead was clear, but the battle was far from over.

As they neared the entrance to the tree's core, Isaac felt a strange sensation—a pulsing energy emanating from the ground beneath them, like the heartbeat of something ancient and alive. The tree knew they were coming. It could feel them, sense their intent. And it wasn't going to let them in without a fight.

Isaac glanced back at the others, his eyes meeting Lydia's. She nodded, her expression resolute. "This is it," she said. "We have to finish this."

Isaac nodded, turning his gaze toward the entrance to the core. It was a massive, gnarled opening in the earth, surrounded by twisted roots that pulsed with dark energy. The core was close—so close that Isaac could feel the tree's malevolent will pressing against him, trying to push him back, trying to stop him.

But they had come too far to turn back now.

Kellar's sacrifice had bought them this chance, and they couldn't let it slip away.

"We go in," Isaac said, his voice steady despite the fear gnawing at him. "We end this."

With a final glance at the spot where Kellar had fallen, Isaac led the group forward, into the heart of the tree

Discovering the Tree's Weakness

The air inside the tree's core was thick with an oppressive, otherworldly energy, a feeling that seemed to pulse through the very ground Isaac walked on. He led the group deeper into the heart of the tree's defenses, every step heavier than the last. His breath came in ragged gasps, the weight of the atmosphere pressing down on him as the tree's ancient power seemed to grow stronger the closer they got to its core.

The survivors—soldiers from the **Inquisition**, remnants of the **Underground Resistance**, and a few battle-hardened sorcerers—moved in silence behind Isaac, their faces pale but determined. They had come too far to turn back now. The losses had been devastating, but this was their last chance. With **Kellar** gone, the group felt more fragile than ever, but Kellar's sacrifice had bought them this opportunity. They couldn't let it slip away.

Isaac could feel the tree's awareness pressing against his mind, probing, searching for weakness. The tree knew they were coming. It was ancient, powerful, and it had adapted to every tactic they had thrown at it. But thanks to **Dr. Martinez** and the research group, they finally had something the tree couldn't adapt to—its vulnerability.

The data they had recovered from the shattered remains of the research base had given them crucial insight into the tree's root system. The tree wasn't just a biological entity; it was something far more complex, something that fed on the very fabric of reality itself. Its roots stretched deep into the earth, anchoring it to the physical world, but they did more than just hold it in place—they were the source of its power. They were drawing energy from something deeper, something older, and that was its weakness.

Isaac's mind raced as he remembered the final moments of Dr. Martinez's analysis before the first assault. "The core is protected by the roots," she had said, pointing to the holographic projection of the tree's root system. "But there are fractures, weak points where the energy is more volatile. If we can plant the charges in those locations, we can destabilize the entire system."

It had been a gamble from the start, but now, standing at the threshold of the tree's heart, Isaac knew it was the only plan they had left. The charges they had prepared, designed using a combination of ancient sorcery and salvaged technology, were specifically calibrated to disrupt the energy the roots were drawing from. If they could plant them in the right places, they could sever the tree's connection to its core, cutting off its ability to regenerate and adapt.

"We're getting close," Martinez said, her voice strained but steady as she walked beside Isaac. She held a device in her hands, a small scanner that was mapping the structure of the roots around them. The device beeped faintly, the readings spiking the closer they got to the core. "The roots here are more exposed. The energy is fluctuating."

Isaac nodded, his eyes scanning the massive, gnarled roots that twisted and curled around them like the limbs of some enormous beast. The deeper they went, the more the roots seemed to pulse with dark energy, glowing faintly in the dim light of the cavern. The air buzzed with the unnatural hum of the tree's influence, and every step felt like a battle against the pull of the tree's will.

"This is it," Lydia said, her voice barely above a whisper. She pointed ahead, to a massive cluster of roots that formed a protective barrier around a glowing, pulsating mass at the center of the cavern—the tree's **core**.

The core wasn't what Isaac had expected. It wasn't just a physical structure, but a swirling mass of dark, churning energy, glowing with a malevolent light that seemed to pulse in time with the tree's roots. It felt alive, aware, watching them.

Isaac's heart raced as he stared at the core. This was the source of the tree's power, the very heart of the nightmare that had consumed the world. If they could destroy it, if they could sever the connection, then maybe—just maybe—they could end this.

Martinez's scanner beeped again, louder this time, the readings spiking as she moved closer to the core. "The fractures are here," she said, her voice filled with a mixture of awe and fear. "The energy is unstable. If we can plant the charges at these points, we can destabilize the core and cut off its power."

Lydia stepped forward, her face set with determination. "Then let's do it."

Setting the Plan in Motion

The group moved quickly, despite the overwhelming pressure of the tree's presence bearing down on them. They had rehearsed the plan back at the base, but now, standing in the heart of the tree, everything felt more immediate, more dangerous.

Martinez and the remaining scientists from her team guided the group to the weak points in the root system. The fractures were faint, barely visible to the naked eye, but the scanner picked them up, mapping out the exact locations where the charges needed to be placed. The charges were small, cylindrical devices that hummed with the energy of the sorcery that powered them. The Inquisition's sorcerers had designed them to disrupt the flow of energy through the roots, severing the connection between the tree and the core.

Isaac took one of the charges from Martinez, his hands shaking slightly as he moved toward the first fracture. The root beneath his feet pulsed with dark energy, and he could feel the tree's awareness pushing against him, trying to stop him. But he pressed on, kneeling beside the root and carefully placing the charge in the small crevice that had formed along the fracture line.

"First charge set," Isaac said, his voice tense.

Lydia nodded, moving to the next location with one of the charges. The others followed suit, each of them working quickly to place the charges at the weak points in the root system. But as they worked, Isaac couldn't shake the feeling that something was wrong. The air around them was growing heavier, the hum of the tree's power growing louder, more insistent.

The tree knew what they were doing.

"We need to move faster," Isaac urged, his eyes darting toward the core. The dark energy swirling within it was becoming more violent, churning like a storm, as if the tree was reacting to their presence, trying to defend itself.

Martinez's hands shook as she placed the final charge, sweat dripping down her forehead. "That's the last one," she said, her voice trembling. "We're ready."

Isaac's heart raced as he stood up, looking at the charges now embedded in the roots. They had done it—they had planted the charges, and if the plan worked, they would sever the tree's connection to its core.

But then, the ground beneath them began to tremble, a low, rumbling vibration that grew stronger with each passing second.

Isaac's eyes widened in horror as he looked around. The roots were pulsing with energy, glowing brighter and brighter as the core began to react. The tree wasn't just going to let them destroy it—it was going to fight back.

"We need to detonate now!" Isaac shouted, his voice rising above the roar of the trembling ground. "Do it!"

Lydia nodded, her hands moving quickly to activate the remote detonator. But as she reached for it, the ground erupted beneath them, and a massive root shot up from the earth, twisting toward the group with terrifying speed.

Isaac barely had time to react. He threw himself to the side, rolling out of the way as the root crashed down, splintering the ground where he had just been standing. The others scattered, dodging the massive tendrils of the tree as they lashed out, trying to stop them.

"The tree's fighting back!" Martinez screamed, her voice filled with panic.

Isaac scrambled to his feet, his heart pounding in his chest. They had to get out of here before the tree tore them apart. The charges were set, but they wouldn't mean anything if they didn't survive long enough to detonate them.

"Lydia, now!" Isaac shouted, his voice hoarse with fear.

Lydia's hands moved in a blur as she activated the detonator. For a split second, there was nothing—just the deafening roar of the tree and the pulsing energy of the core.

And then, the charges went off.

The ground shook violently as the explosions rippled through the root system, sending shockwaves through the cavern. The roots convulsed, the energy within them flickering and dimming as the charges severed the flow of power. The core, once a swirling mass of dark energy, flickered and sputtered, its light growing dimmer.

Isaac watched in awe as the tree's power began to unravel, its connection to the core weakening. They had done it. They had found the tree's weakness.

But even as the core flickered, Isaac knew the battle wasn't over yet. The tree was still alive, and it would not go down without a fight.

CHAPTER 28

The Last Stand

The cavern shook violently as the explosions from the charges rippled through the ground. Isaac stumbled, barely managing to keep his footing as the world around him seemed to convulse in pain. The roots of the tree, once pulsing with an eerie, malevolent energy, now writhed and twisted in agony, their connection to the core severed by the carefully placed charges. But despite the damage they had inflicted, the tree was far from defeated.

Isaac's chest heaved with exhaustion as he looked around at the chaos unfolding around him. The air was thick with dust and the acrid scent of burning roots, and the low, ominous hum of the tree's influence seemed to grow louder, angrier. It was as though the tree was lashing out in its death throes, desperate to hold onto the power that had sustained it for so long.

"We did it," Isaac muttered, his voice barely audible over the roar of the collapsing roots. But there was no time for relief. The tree's core, now flickering and sputtering in the center of the cavern, was still alive. Its energy was unstable, churning violently as it fought to maintain its grip on reality. The battle was far from over.

"We need to keep moving!" Lydia's voice cut through the noise, sharp and commanding. She was already pushing forward, her eyes locked on the tree's core. "The core is weakened, but it's not destroyed. We have to finish this!"

Isaac nodded, his muscles screaming in protest as he forced himself to follow her. Around them, the remaining soldiers and sorcerers struggled to regroup. The explosions had shaken the battlefield, and many had been thrown to the ground by the force of the blast. But the survivors were already getting back to their feet, their faces grim with determination. They knew what was at stake. This was their last chance, and they couldn't afford to falter now.

As they moved deeper into the cavern, Isaac could feel the weight of the tree's influence pressing down on him, heavier than ever before. The air itself seemed to throb with dark energy, and every step felt like wading through quicksand. The tree wasn't just reacting to the damage they had done—it was fighting back, trying to drag them into its twisted reality. Time seemed to warp and bend around them, the cavern stretching and distorting as if the tree was trying to pull them apart, to tear them from their goal.

"Stay together!" Kellar's second-in-command, **Damon**, shouted, his voice barely audible over the noise. He had taken up leadership of the Resistance after Kellar's death, though the burden of command weighed heavily on him. Isaac could see the grief in his eyes, the exhaustion that seemed to radiate from every movement. But Damon hadn't hesitated. Despite the losses, despite the overwhelming odds, he had stepped up and kept the Resistance fighting.

The group pressed forward, their pace slowing as the ground beneath them became more treacherous. Massive roots, now severed from their source of power, had begun to collapse inward, creating a labyrinth of obstacles that they had to navigate. The air was thick with dust and debris, making it hard to see more than a few feet ahead. But Isaac could still make out the faint glow of the core in the distance, pulsing with a sickly light.

Just as they neared the final stretch toward the core, a blood-curdling scream echoed through the cavern. Isaac's heart lurched as he turned to see one of the Resistance fighters dragged into the shadows by a massive, writhing root. The aberrations were still here, still fighting to defend the tree. Their grotesque forms, twisted and unnatural, emerged from the darkness, their many eyes gleaming with hunger as they lunged at the group.

"They're coming!" someone shouted, and the sound of gunfire and sorcery filled the air once more.

Isaac raised his weapon, firing into the mass of aberrations as they charged toward them. The creatures were relentless, moving with a speed and ferocity that Isaac hadn't seen before. It was as if the tree's desperation had infected them, driving them into a frenzy.

One of the aberrations, a hulking beast covered in spiked, writhing limbs, barreled toward Isaac. He fired at it, but the creature shrugged off the bullets as if they were nothing. Isaac barely managed to dodge as the creature swung one of its massive limbs at him, the force of the blow sending him sprawling to the ground. He rolled to the side, just in time to avoid being impaled by the creature's spikes, and scrambled to his feet.

Lydia stepped forward, her hands glowing with the power of her sorcery. She raised her arms, and a blinding bolt of energy shot from her fingertips, striking the creature square in the chest. The aberration let out a deafening screech as the energy coursed through its body, its limbs convulsing violently before it collapsed to the ground, dead.

But there was no time to celebrate. More aberrations were closing in, their grotesque forms slithering through the wreckage of the roots as they attacked with a renewed fury. Isaac fired into the swarm, but for every creature that fell, more seemed to take its place. The tree's influence was everywhere, warping the battlefield, twisting reality itself.

"We're losing people!" Damon shouted, his voice filled with desperation. Isaac turned to see more Resistance fighters being overwhelmed, dragged into the shadows by the aberrations. The losses were mounting, and the group was shrinking with every passing moment.

Isaac's heart pounded in his chest as he realized how close they were to failure. The core was right in front of them, but the tree was defending it with everything it had left. If they couldn't break through, if they couldn't reach the core...

"Keep moving!" Lydia shouted, her voice hoarse but resolute. She blasted another aberration with a burst of energy, her hands trembling with the strain. "We're almost there!"

Isaac gritted his teeth, his body aching with exhaustion as he pushed forward. The core was so close now, glowing with a sickly light that flickered like a dying flame. But the aberrations were everywhere, cutting down more of their group with every step. Isaac could hear the screams of the dying, could feel the weight of every life lost, but he couldn't stop. Not now.

With a final surge of effort, Isaac and the remaining survivors broke through the last line of aberrations, reaching the base of the core. It pulsed with a strange, almost hypnotic rhythm, as if it was trying to draw them in, to pull them into its twisted reality. Isaac could feel the tree's influence pressing against his mind, trying to worm its way inside, but he fought it off, focusing on the task at hand.

"The charges!" Lydia shouted, her voice strained. "We have to plant the charges!"

Isaac nodded, pulling the remaining charges from his pack. His hands shook as he placed the first charge at the base of the core, the dark energy swirling around him as he worked. The air felt thick, oppressive, as if the tree itself was trying to smother them.

One by one, the others planted their charges around the core, their movements frantic but precise. The core flickered violently, the dark energy within it growing more unstable with each charge that was set.

"We've got them all!" Damon called out, his face slick with sweat. "Now we just need to—"

A massive root shot up from the ground, wrapping around Damon's legs and yanking him into the air. He screamed, firing his weapon wildly as the root pulled him toward the core. Isaac watched in horror as Damon was dragged closer to the pulsating mass of energy, his screams echoing through the cavern.

Without thinking, Isaac lunged forward, grabbing hold of Damon's arm. He pulled with all his strength, but the root was too strong, too fast. Isaac's grip slipped, and with one final, agonizing scream, Damon was pulled into the core, disappearing into the swirling darkness.

Isaac stumbled back, his heart racing. Damon was gone. Another life lost to the tree. And now it was just him and Lydia, the last survivors of their group.

"Detonate the charges!" Lydia shouted, her voice filled with a mixture of fury and desperation.

Isaac's hands trembled as he reached for the detonator. The core was flickering wildly now, the energy inside it growing more and more unstable. The charges were in place. This was it.

With a deep breath, Isaac pressed the button.

The explosion was instantaneous, a blinding flash of light that tore through the cavern. The ground shook violently, and Isaac was thrown to the ground as the core erupted in a shower of energy. The tree's roots convulsed, writhing in agony as the energy was severed, the core collapsing in on itself.

Isaac lay on the ground, his ears ringing, his vision blurred. He could feel the weight of the tree's influence lifting, the oppressive energy dissipating as the core was destroyed. The battle was over.

But the cost had been immense.

The Fall of the Tree

The aftermath of the explosion rippled through the air, a blinding flash of energy that turned the sky a burning white before collapsing into a heavy silence. Isaac lay on the ground, dazed, his body aching as he struggled to understand what had just happened. The core of the tree—the pulsating heart of its nightmarish power—had imploded, taking with it the dense web of roots that had anchored it to the earth. The tremors in the ground had stopped, the oppressive hum of the tree's influence had dissipated, and for the first time in what felt like an eternity, the world was quiet.

But Isaac's heart was still pounding, his chest tight as he forced himself to sit up. His vision was blurry, and the air was thick with dust and debris, swirling in the aftermath of the destruction. Around him, the battlefield was eerily still. What had moments ago been a frenzied clash of life and death had now fallen into an unsettling calm.

He could see the twisted remains of the tree, its once massive and imposing form reduced to a crumbling skeleton of withered roots and shattered bark. The explosion had ripped through its core, severing the connections that had allowed it to feed on the world. The aberrations that had defended it had vanished—either destroyed in the blast or lost without the tree to sustain them.

But despite the victory, there was no sense of triumph. Isaac knew, deep down, that this was not the end of their suffering.

Isaac struggled to his feet, every muscle aching with the weight of exhaustion and grief. His mind raced, but his body moved on instinct, stumbling through the rubble, searching for signs of life. He spotted **Lydia**, not far from where he had fallen, leaning against a crumbled root. Her face was streaked with dirt and blood, but she was alive. She met Isaac's gaze, her eyes reflecting the same hollow realization that he felt deep in his bones.

"It's over," Lydia said, her voice barely audible. "The tree… it's gone."

Isaac nodded, but his throat tightened as he looked around. The cost had been immense. The tree's fall, while necessary, had come at a price too great to bear. The lives lost—the friends, the fighters, the survivors—they all weighed heavily on his soul. Isaac could still see the faces of those who had died, their sacrifices fresh in his mind, and now, as he stood among the wreckage, the overwhelming burden of it all crashed down on him.

"Where is everyone?" Isaac asked, his voice trembling. He staggered toward Lydia, his legs feeling like they might give out at any moment.

Lydia grimaced, her hand pressing against her side where a dark stain of blood had spread across her jacket. "We lost too many. Damon… he's gone. Kellar, Martinez, all of them. We're the last ones."

The words hit Isaac like a physical blow, the reality of their situation sinking in. He had known the losses were heavy, but hearing it spoken aloud felt like a final nail in the coffin. He looked around at the desolation, seeing the remains of the battlefield littered with the bodies of those who had fought to bring the tree down. The few survivors moved like shadows in the distance, silent and aimless, their hope stripped away with the destruction of the tree.

Isaac felt an ache deep in his chest, the kind that went beyond physical pain. He had led them here—led them into this fight, into this nightmare—and now all that remained were echoes of what could have been. Victory had been their only option, and they had achieved it, but the price was too much to bear.

"We did it," Isaac said, his voice hollow. "We stopped it, but… what now?"

Lydia pushed herself upright, her face tight with pain as she moved closer to Isaac. "We rebuild, if there's anything left to rebuild. We can't let everything we lost be for nothing. We have to move forward, somehow."

Isaac looked at her, trying to find solace in her words, but the enormity of the situation felt suffocating. The tree had been destroyed, but the world they had fought to save was in ruins. The ground beneath them had been torn apart by the tree's influence, and the sky—though no longer filled with the red glow of the tree's corruption—was still a sickly gray, thick with the residue of the explosion.

They were standing in the aftermath of the greatest battle humanity had ever faced, but Isaac couldn't shake the feeling that the world had already been lost.

The Cost of Victory

As Isaac and Lydia made their way through the debris, they passed the remains of what had once been their comrades-in-arms. The bodies of the Resistance fighters, the Inquisition soldiers, and even some of the sorcerers lay strewn across the battlefield, their faces frozen in expressions of pain and defiance. These were the people who had believed in the fight, who had given everything they had to destroy the tree. But now, with the battle over, their sacrifice felt like a hollow victory.

Isaac's thoughts turned to **Kellar**, whose rage and determination had carried them this far. He had died for this cause, driven by his hatred for the tree and what it had taken from him. And **Damon**, who had stepped into Kellar's shoes, had been dragged into the tree's core, disappearing in its final moments. Their deaths, like so many others, weighed on Isaac like an unbearable burden.

"Was it worth it?" Isaac whispered, his voice breaking. "Was it worth all this?"

Lydia didn't answer at first. She looked out over the devastated landscape, her expression unreadable. When she finally spoke, her voice was low, filled with both resolve and sorrow. "It had to be. If we hadn't fought, the tree would have consumed everything. But I don't know what's left for us now."

They continued walking in silence, the enormity of what they had lost sinking in with every step. The ground beneath them was scorched, twisted by the tree's influence, and the air felt thick with an unnatural heaviness that refused to lift, even after the core had been destroyed. Isaac could see the remnants of cities in the distance, their broken silhouettes jutting out against the horizon like monuments to a world that no longer existed.

The survivors they encountered were few and far between. Some wandered aimlessly, their eyes vacant as they processed the aftermath of the battle. Others knelt beside the fallen, mourning silently. There were no cheers of victory, no triumphant celebration. The cost had been too great for anyone to feel anything but grief.

A Changed World

As the hours passed, Isaac and Lydia reached the outskirts of what had once been a city. The buildings were crumbling, overtaken by the tree's roots, but without the energy from the core to sustain them, the roots had withered and died. The city was a shell of its former self, a reminder of the world that had been left behind in the wake of the tree's rise to power.

"This place…" Lydia said, her voice trailing off as she looked at the ruins. "It's all gone, isn't it?"

Isaac didn't respond. He didn't have the words to express the devastation he felt. The world had been forever changed by the tree's influence, and there was no going back to the way things had been before. The tree was gone, but the scars it had left behind would never fully heal.

Suddenly, a distant sound broke the silence—a faint, steady hum, almost imperceptible at first, but growing louder with each passing moment. Isaac's heart skipped a beat as he looked up, scanning the horizon for the source of the noise. And then he saw it—a small group of survivors, making their way toward them, their figures barely visible against the ruined landscape.

For the first time since the explosion, Isaac felt a flicker of something—hope.

"We're not alone," he murmured, his voice filled with cautious relief.

Lydia looked up, following his gaze. She smiled, a faint, tired smile that carried with it the weight of everything they had been through. "No," she said softly. "We're not."

The survivors approached, their faces worn but determined. They were a reminder that, despite everything, life went on. The world was broken, but there were still people left to rebuild it. They had lost so much, but they hadn't lost everything.

Isaac took a deep breath, the weight on his shoulders lightening just a little. The battle had been won, but the fight to rebuild their world was just beginning.

And maybe, just maybe, there was still hope.

CHAPTER 30
Pyrrhic Victory

Isaac stood atop a hill of rubble, gazing out over the shattered landscape that stretched for miles in every direction. The world lay in ruins, broken and twisted by the tree's influence, its once-vibrant life now a distant memory. The air was still heavy with the scent of smoke and decay, and the faint, ever-present hum of the tree's energy seemed to linger, like the ghost of a nightmare that refused to fully release its grip on reality. Despite their victory, Isaac couldn't shake the feeling that the battle wasn't truly over.

The **blood-red moon** hung high in the sky, casting its eerie glow over the devastation below. It hadn't returned to its natural state, hadn't faded into the familiar pale white of peace. Instead, it seemed to loom over the world like a grim reminder of the horrors they had faced, a symbol of the tree's lingering influence. Isaac stared at it for a long time, the weight of the past months pressing down on him like a heavy shroud. He wondered if the moon would ever return to normal—or if it would remain as it was, a permanent scar in the sky, marking this broken world.

The remnants of the tree's destruction were everywhere. The once-massive trunk that had dominated the landscape was now reduced to a skeletal husk, charred and crumbling. Its roots, which had once dug deep into the earth, warping the land with their dark power, were now nothing more than brittle, withered tendrils, slowly disintegrating in the cold air. But even in its defeat, the tree's presence lingered. The ground beneath Isaac's feet still felt unstable, as if the world itself hadn't quite recovered from the trauma of the battle.

"We won," Isaac whispered to himself, though the words felt hollow.

He glanced over his shoulder at the survivors gathered behind him—what few remained. **Lydia** was among them, her face drawn with exhaustion and grief. They had all lost so much. Friends, allies, the lives they had known before the tree emerged and tore everything apart. They had fought for this victory, bled for it, but standing in the aftermath, it was impossible to feel like they had truly won.

Lydia approached him, her footsteps slow and deliberate, as if she, too, was struggling under the weight of everything they had endured. She stopped beside him, her gaze drifting out over the ruined landscape. "It doesn't feel like it's over, does it?"

Isaac shook his head, his eyes still fixed on the distant horizon. "No. It feels like we stopped one nightmare, but we've woken up to another."

They stood in silence for a moment, the enormity of the destruction sinking in. Cities lay in ruins, their once-proud structures toppled like the trees in a forest fire. Roads were torn apart, twisted by the roots that had surged up from the earth during the tree's reign. The sky, still tinted a sickly red from the blood moon, made the world feel otherworldly, as if they were walking through a dream from which they couldn't wake.

Isaac's mind wandered back to those who had fallen—**Kellar**, whose rage had driven him to sacrifice himself in the heat of battle; **Damon**, who had been dragged into the core, lost to the tree in its final moments; **Dr. Martinez**, whose brilliant mind had fought so hard to find the answers that might have saved them. Their deaths weighed heavily on Isaac, and he knew that, despite the tree's destruction, the world would never be the same.

"It's hard to know where to start," Lydia said softly, her voice carrying a hint of the sorrow she was trying to keep at bay. "We've lost so much."

Isaac nodded, the lump in his throat making it difficult to speak. "We didn't just lose people. We lost… everything. The world we fought for isn't here anymore."

The silence between them deepened, the gravity of his words sinking in. They had fought to save the world, but now, standing in the ruins, it was clear that the world they had known was gone. The tree's influence had infected more than just the land—it had left its mark on the very fabric of reality. The sky was still wrong. The moon was still red. And even the few plants and animals that remained had been twisted and altered by the tree's dark power.

"Do you think it'll ever go back to how it was?" Lydia asked, her voice barely above a whisper.

Isaac wanted to give her some reassurance, wanted to tell her that they would rebuild, that the world would heal, but he couldn't bring himself to say the words. Instead, he shook his head. "I don't know. I think… we're going to have to live with this."

Lydia let out a long breath, her shoulders slumping with the weight of the realization. "Maybe you're right. But we're still here, Isaac. That has to count for something."

Isaac turned to look at her, the tired but unwavering determination in her eyes. He knew she was right. They were still alive. They had survived. And maybe that was enough, for now.

They started making their way back toward the others, the survivors gathered in small groups, their faces worn and haunted. There were whispers of what to do next, of how to rebuild in a world that had been so thoroughly shattered. But there was no clear plan. There was only uncertainty.

As they reached the others, Isaac saw that a few of the **Inquisition sorcerers** were standing together, their hands outstretched as they examined the tree's remains. Their faces were drawn with concern, and Isaac could hear the faint murmur of their conversation. He approached them cautiously, his curiosity piqued by the strange symbols they were tracing in the air.

"What is it?" Isaac asked, his voice low.

One of the sorcerers, a man with deep-set eyes and a weary expression, glanced up at him. "It's the residual energy," he said, his voice tinged with unease. "The tree is gone, but its influence... it's still here. We can feel it in the ground, in the air. It's like the tree left something behind."

Isaac frowned, a sense of dread creeping into his chest. "What do you mean? We destroyed the core."

The sorcerer nodded. "Yes, but the tree was ancient, tied to something deeper than just its physical form. It was connected to this world in ways we don't fully understand. Its destruction severed that connection, but the energy it left behind... it's still here, lingering. It may take years—decades—for it to fully dissipate."

Isaac felt a chill run down his spine. Even in death, the tree wasn't gone. Its presence would haunt the earth for years to come, its influence a permanent scar on the landscape. He glanced up at the blood-red moon once more, its ominous glow casting long shadows over the land.

"Will it ever be gone?" Isaac asked, his voice barely above a whisper.

The sorcerer hesitated for a moment, then shook his head. "I don't know. We'll do what we can, but... this world has been changed forever."

Isaac stared at the ground, the weight of the sorcerer's words settling over him like a heavy blanket. He had hoped—foolishly, perhaps—that destroying the tree would mean a fresh start, a chance to rebuild what had been lost. But now, he realized that there would be no clean slate. The world was irrevocably altered, and they would have to live with the consequences of the battle for the rest of their lives.

The New World

As the sun began to set, the survivors gathered together, sharing what little supplies they had left. There was no celebration, no fanfare. Only quiet conversation and weary glances as they took stock of what remained. The destruction of the tree had left them all broken in some way, and now they faced the daunting task of rebuilding in a world that had been so profoundly scarred.

Isaac sat apart from the others, his back against a fallen chunk of the tree's massive trunk. His mind was a swirl of conflicting emotions—grief for the lives lost, relief that the tree was finally destroyed, and a deep, gnawing uncertainty about the future. The victory had come at a staggering cost, and now they had to find a way to move forward.

As the sky darkened and the blood-red moon rose higher, casting its eerie light over the land, Isaac closed his eyes and let out a long, slow breath.

The battle was over. The tree had fallen.

But the world they had fought to save would never be the same.

Grieving and Reflection

Isaac sat alone by the remnants of a smoldering fire, the quiet crackle of the last burning embers providing a small sense of warmth in the cool night air. The blood-red moon still hung high in the sky, its ominous glow casting long shadows over the broken landscape. Though the tree had fallen, the weight of their victory pressed heavily on his shoulders. The world had survived, but at what cost? The battle was over, but the true struggle—grappling with the loss of so many lives, the destruction of everything they once knew—was only just beginning.

Isaac's eyes burned with exhaustion, but sleep wouldn't come. Every time he closed his eyes, the faces of the fallen returned to him. **Kellar**, whose rage had driven him to sacrifice himself. **Damon**, who had been swallowed by the core in the final moments of the battle. **Dr. Martinez**, whose brilliant mind had been lost in the chaos. And all the nameless others who had fought and died to bring down the tree.

The survivors were scattered around the campsite, quietly tending to their wounds and sharing what little food and water they had. There was no celebration, no sense of relief—only grief, exhaustion, and a lingering sense of guilt. Isaac could see it in their faces. They had won, but it didn't feel like a victory.

He stared at the tattered remnants of his old backpack, barely holding together after all that had happened. Inside, buried beneath supplies and gear, was the **Vagabond's Diary**. Isaac hadn't looked at it in days, too consumed by the battle to focus on anything else. But now, as the silence stretched on, the urge to open it, to read the final entry, gnawed at him.

With a heavy sigh, Isaac reached into the pack and pulled out the leather-bound book, its pages worn and stained from the months of travel. The diary had been his guide in many ways, a dark reflection of his own journey through the nightmare that the tree had created. Each entry had brought him closer to understanding the world they had been thrown into, and now, in the aftermath of the battle, he felt compelled to see how the vagabond's story ended.

He flipped through the pages, his fingers tracing the familiar handwriting as he read through the earlier entries, memories of his own experiences flooding back. The destruction, the loss, the moments of fleeting hope—all of it was reflected in the vagabond's words. Finally, he reached the last entry, the ink faded but still legible. Isaac took a deep breath and began to read.

Vagabond's Diary – Final Entry

"I've wandered through the ruins of cities, through forests twisted by the tree's power, and through landscapes that no longer follow the rules of nature. I've seen people lost to madness, their minds shattered by the nightmares the tree forces upon them. I've seen entire towns swallowed by its roots, their inhabitants consumed by something far worse than death."

"And yet, I keep walking. I keep searching. For what, I don't know. Perhaps it's hope. Perhaps it's an answer. But each step feels heavier than the last, as if the weight of the world itself is pressing down on me. The tree... it is everywhere. Even when I am far from its reach, I can feel its presence, lurking in the shadows, whispering in the wind. It's like it knows I'm still here. Like it's watching me."

"I've met others along the way. Some still fight, still believe they can stop it. I want to believe them. I want to think that there's still a way to end this, to take back what the tree has stolen from us. But the more I see, the more I begin to

doubt. The tree isn't just a thing. It's a force, a wound in the fabric of the world, and wounds like this don't just heal. They fester."

"Maybe that's what the tree really is—an infection. It took root in the world, and now it's spreading, slowly, methodically, changing everything it touches. And I... I am just one person. What can I do against something so vast, so powerful?"

"I've lost so much. I've lost friends, allies, and people I barely knew. The tree took them all, and it will take me too, eventually. I can feel it, in my bones, in my mind. It's creeping into my thoughts, pulling me into its darkness. I don't know how much longer I can resist."

"But if there's one thing I've learned on this journey, it's that you can't stop fighting. Even when everything seems lost, even when the world is crumbling around you, you have to keep going. Because if you stop, if you give in to the tree's whispers, then it's already won."

"So I keep walking. I don't know where this path will lead me, but I will follow it until the end. And if I fall, if the tree finally takes me, then at least I can say I didn't stop. I didn't give up. Not until the very last step."

Isaac stared at the final words, his chest tightening with emotion. The vagabond's journey, so similar to his own, had been one of constant struggle, constant loss. And yet, despite everything, the vagabond had kept walking, kept fighting, even when hope seemed impossible. Isaac could feel the weight of those words pressing down on him, resonating with the grief and guilt that had settled deep in his heart.

The diary had been a reflection of his own path, a dark mirror of the journey he had taken to reach this point. Like the vagabond, Isaac had lost so much—his friends, his allies, the world he had known—and yet, he had kept fighting. Even when the tree's influence seemed unstoppable, when the odds were stacked against them, he had refused to give up. But now, in the aftermath of the battle, he wasn't sure if it had been enough.

"We did everything we could," Lydia's voice came softly from behind him, breaking the silence. She had seen him reading the diary and approached quietly, her face etched with the same exhaustion and grief that weighed on him. "You know that, right?"

Isaac didn't respond immediately. He closed the diary, his hands shaking slightly as he placed it back in his pack. "I know," he said finally, his voice strained. "But it doesn't make it any easier. We won, but... look at what's left. Look at what we lost."

Lydia sat down beside him, her gaze distant as she looked out over the ruins. "I've been thinking about that a lot. About whether it was worth it. But the truth is... we didn't have a choice. If we hadn't fought, the tree would've consumed everything. We had to stop it, even if it cost us everything."

Isaac nodded slowly, though the weight of his guilt still lingered. He thought about **Kellar's** sacrifice, the way Damon had been swallowed by the core, the losses that had piled up along the way. He had led them into this fight, and now, standing in the ruins, he wondered if there had been another way— some way to save more lives, to avoid so much pain.

"I keep thinking about them," Isaac murmured, his voice barely audible. "Kellar, Damon, all of them. I can't help but feel like I failed them."

"You didn't," Lydia said firmly, turning to face him. "They made their choices. We all did. We knew what we were up against, and we fought because we believed it was the only way. Kellar's rage, Damon's hope... they drove them, just like your determination drove you. But none of us could have predicted how it would end."

Isaac swallowed hard, his throat tight. "I just... I thought it would feel different. Winning."

Lydia sighed, her eyes softening with understanding. "I know. So did I. But this... this is the cost. Victory doesn't always look like we imagined."

They sat in silence for a long time, the sounds of the wind rustling through the broken branches of the dead tree filling the air. The final entry in the **Vagabond's Diary** lingered in Isaac's mind, a haunting echo of his own journey. Like the vagabond, he had walked through the nightmare, fought against impossible odds, and now, standing on the other side, he wasn't sure what came next.

But one thing was clear—he hadn't given up. Not until the very end.

CHAPTER 32

Uncertainty

The sky above was still painted in deep shades of red, though the intensity had lessened since the tree fell. The blood-red moon, once a constant reminder of the tree's dominion, still hung in the sky, casting its eerie light over the devastated landscape. Its glow seemed softer now, less menacing, but the sight of it filled Isaac with unease. The tree was gone—destroyed in a final, massive explosion of energy—but the moon's lingering presence raised questions Isaac couldn't shake.

He stood alone on the outskirts of the shattered battlefield, his thoughts swirling like the dust that still clung to the air. The survivors had begun to gather what remained of their supplies, trying to make sense of what came next. There were whispers of rebuilding, of finding safe places to start over. But Isaac wasn't sure if they truly had something to rebuild—or if the world had simply entered a new, unfamiliar darkness.

He had spent the last hours in quiet reflection, trying to process everything that had happened. The battle had been brutal, the losses immeasurable. The tree had been the source of their nightmare, but its roots had run deeper than they'd ever realized. The destruction of the tree had felt like a moment of release, but now, standing in its wake, Isaac wasn't sure if they had won—or if they had simply delayed the inevitable.

The land around him was still scarred. The tree's roots, though severed and withered, still clung to the earth like the skeletal remains of a long-dead giant. The ground itself felt wrong beneath his feet, as though it had been fundamentally changed by the tree's presence. The air was thick, not just with dust, but with something more—an invisible tension that Isaac could feel with every breath.

It was as though the tree had left behind a piece of itself, a stain on the world that wouldn't wash away. Despite its destruction, Isaac couldn't shake the feeling that the tree's influence wasn't truly gone. It was just… hiding, waiting for the right moment to return.

But maybe that was just the fear talking.

Isaac ran a hand through his tangled hair, feeling the weight of his exhaustion deep in his bones. The blood-red moon loomed above, a constant reminder of the unknown. Was it still a symbol of the tree's power, or had it simply become part of the damaged sky? He didn't know. And that uncertainty gnawed at him.

He turned and made his way back to where the others were gathered. **Lydia** was there, talking quietly with a small group of survivors, their faces pale and gaunt. They had fought through hell and back, and now, they were left with nothing but the uncertain future ahead of them. Isaac knew they looked to him for answers, for guidance, but he wasn't sure if he had any left to give.

As he approached, Lydia glanced up and caught his eye. She excused herself from the group and made her way over to him, her expression as weary as his own. For a long moment, neither of them spoke. They just stood there, taking in the silence that had fallen over the land, the quiet that felt too fragile to last.

"You look like you've got the weight of the world on your shoulders," Lydia said softly, a faint smile tugging at her lips, though there was no real humor in it.

Isaac shrugged, his gaze drifting back to the horizon. "I guess I do. Or what's left of it, anyway."

Lydia followed his gaze, her eyes narrowing slightly as she looked at the blood-red moon. "You think it's really over?"

Isaac was silent for a long time, unsure of how to answer. The truth was, he didn't know. The tree was gone, yes, but its mark on the world was unmistakable. The land was still twisted and broken, the moon still burned red, and the survivors were left picking up the pieces of a life they barely recognized. Was this truly the end of the nightmare, or had they just entered a new one?

"I don't know," Isaac said finally, his voice low. "We destroyed the tree, but… look around. The world's still broken. And that moon—it's still there. Still red."

Lydia sighed, her shoulders slumping slightly. "I've been thinking the same thing. It doesn't feel like a victory. Not really. More like… like we just stopped one phase of this nightmare."

Isaac nodded, her words echoing the thoughts that had been swirling in his mind. The battle had ended, but the sense of foreboding hadn't lifted. It was as if the world itself had been fundamentally altered, and there was no going back to the way things had been before. The tree's influence had sunk too deeply into the fabric of reality, warping the land, the sky, and even the people who had survived.

"We fought so hard to stop it," Isaac said, his voice tightening with frustration. "But what if this is it? What if the world doesn't go back to normal? What if the tree… changed everything permanently?"

Lydia glanced at him, her expression thoughtful. "It's possible. But we don't know what the future holds, Isaac. Maybe the world will heal, slowly. Maybe it won't ever be the same, but we'll find a way to live in it."

"Or maybe we're just waiting for something worse," Isaac muttered.

Lydia frowned. "We can't think like that. We can't live in constant fear of what might happen. If we do, then we've already lost. We've survived this long, Isaac. We have to believe that there's still a chance, even if it's small."

Isaac wanted to believe her, wanted to cling to the hope that they had fought for something greater than just delaying another catastrophe. But the uncertainty gnawed at him. He had seen the way the tree had twisted the world, the way its roots had burrowed into the earth like a sickness. Could something so deeply embedded ever truly be eradicated?

He looked down at his hands, still stained with dirt and blood from the battle. His fingers trembled slightly, the weight of everything they had fought for pressing down on him. "I don't know if I can do it, Lydia. I don't know if I can keep fighting—if I can face whatever comes next."

Lydia placed a hand on his arm, her touch gentle but firm. "You don't have to face it alone. None of us do. Whatever happens next, we'll face it together."

Isaac nodded, though the uncertainty still lingered. He knew Lydia was right. They weren't alone. The survivors, though few, were still here. And together, they would have to rebuild—find a way to live in this new, broken world. But the question that weighed most heavily on Isaac's mind was whether the world could ever be truly free of the tree's influence.

The blood-red moon hung above them, a constant reminder of the unknown. As Isaac stared up at it, a shiver ran down his spine. It felt like the moon was watching them, just as the tree had once watched from its towering height. Was it a remnant of the tree's power, or was it something else entirely? Isaac couldn't say. And that was what frightened him the most.

"What do we do now?" Isaac asked, his voice barely above a whisper.

Lydia looked at him, her expression somber. "We survive. We rebuild. And we stay vigilant. Whatever comes next, we'll be ready for it."

Isaac nodded, though the uncertainty still gnawed at him. The future was a vast unknown, filled with possibilities—both good and bad. And though the battle had ended, the world had been forever changed. They had survived, but the scars of the tree's reign would never fully heal.

Isaac glanced one last time at the blood-red moon before turning his gaze back to the survivors. They were huddled together, talking quietly, making plans for the days to come. There was fear in their eyes, but also determination. They had faced the nightmare and lived. Now they had to figure out how to live in the wake of it.

"We keep going," Isaac whispered to himself, the words feeling like both a promise and a burden. "We keep going."

The Survivors

The morning light was weak, filtering through the haze of dust and smoke that still clung to the horizon like a shroud. The blood-red moon had finally dipped below the skyline, but its unsettling glow remained fresh in Isaac's mind. The landscape around them was eerily quiet, the usual sounds of life—birds, wind, even the rustle of trees—seemingly absent. Instead, there was only the soft crunch of footsteps as the few remaining survivors gathered near the remains of the battlefield, huddled around small fires to ward off the morning chill.

Isaac stood at a distance, watching them. It was a strange sight—the people who had once been fighters, soldiers, sorcerers, and scientists, now reduced to small clusters of weary survivors trying to make sense of what came next. The battle had been won, but the victory was hollow, overshadowed by the sheer magnitude of what they had lost. There was no joy, no celebration—only the grim reality of a world forever changed.

Lydia approached him, her breath visible in the cold air as she pulled her jacket tighter around her. Her face, like everyone else's, was etched with exhaustion. "They're starting to talk about what to do next," she said softly. "Some want to leave, try to find safer places. Others... they're too scared to move."

Isaac glanced at the survivors again. There weren't many left—just a few dozen, scattered across the ruined landscape like shadows. Some sat in silence, staring into the fires, their eyes empty with the weight of everything they had endured. Others were in hushed conversations, their voices barely rising above whispers as they discussed plans, dreams, or perhaps just shared the horrors of what they had seen.

"I don't blame them for being scared," Isaac said, his voice heavy. "We all are. After everything we've seen, everything we've lost, it's hard to imagine anything going back to normal."

Lydia nodded, her eyes distant. "The world's changed. We don't know what's out there anymore—what's left. People are talking about the tree like it's still here, like it's still… watching."

Isaac frowned, feeling a familiar chill run down his spine. He had felt it too, that lingering sense of something not quite gone. Even with the tree destroyed, its influence still seemed to cling to the land like a stain. It was hard to shake the feeling that they were still being watched, that the nightmare wasn't truly over.

"They're not wrong," Isaac said quietly. "The tree left its mark on the world. We don't know how deep that mark runs. Maybe it'll fade in time, maybe it won't. But right now… it feels like it's still here, in the air, in the ground."

Lydia's gaze drifted across the broken landscape. "Some people are talking about trying to rebuild. They think if we stick together, we can make something out of the ruins. But others… they're ready to leave it all behind."

Isaac sighed. "There's no easy answer. We can't stay here forever, but where do we go? What's left to rebuild when the world we knew is gone?"

They both fell silent, the weight of the question hanging between them. Isaac knew that no matter what they decided, the future was uncertain. The tree's influence had twisted the world in ways they didn't fully understand, and even though the core had been destroyed, its legacy was still very much alive.

A Gathering of Fractured Souls

Later that day, the survivors gathered in what had once been the center of their camp. The remnants of tents and makeshift shelters littered the area, and the air was thick with the smell of burned wood and earth. Isaac, Lydia, and a few others stood at the edge of the group, listening as the conversations ebbed and flowed around them.

There was no formal leader anymore—**Kellar** was gone, and those who had once commanded respect were either dead or too shattered by the battle to step up. Instead, the survivors spoke in turns, each voice offering something different: hope, fear, despair, determination.

One man, a former soldier with deep lines etched into his weathered face, stood and spoke first. "We've fought hard," he said, his voice rough. "We did what we had to do to bring that damn tree down. But now that it's over… what do we have left? This land, these ruins—there's nothing here for us."

He paused, his gaze sweeping over the group. "We need to leave. There's no future in this place. Whatever's out there, it has to be better than staying here, living in the shadow of the tree's remains."

A murmur of agreement rippled through the group, but others remained silent, their expressions uncertain.

A woman named **Anya**, one of the few remaining members of the Inquisition, shook her head. "And where would we go? The world has been twisted by the tree. We don't know what's beyond the horizon. We don't even know if the tree's influence is truly gone. For all we know, it could still be out there, waiting to grow back."

The group fell silent at her words, the gravity of the unknown pressing down on them.

Anya continued, her voice filled with conviction. "I'm not saying we can't rebuild. I'm saying we need to be smart about it. We need to learn from what's happened, understand what the tree did to the world. If we run blindly into the unknown, we could end up in even worse situations."

Isaac felt a pang of agreement with both of them. He could understand the desire to leave, to abandon this place that had been the epicenter of their nightmare. But at the same time, Anya was right—they didn't know what the world looked like beyond this broken horizon. What if the tree's influence hadn't truly ended? What if they were walking into a new kind of danger?

Another voice spoke up—a young man who had been a part of the Underground Resistance, his face pale but determined. "We have to try. I don't know if the tree's gone for good, but I know we can't just stay here, waiting for something worse to come along. We've survived this long. We can survive whatever's out there."

More voices chimed in—some agreeing with the need to leave, others arguing for caution. The debate continued, growing more heated as the survivors tried to make sense of what came next.

Lydia leaned closer to Isaac, her voice low. "What do you think? Should we stay or go?"

Isaac stared into the distance, the ruins of the tree's fallen husk still visible in the background, a reminder of everything they had fought and lost. "I think... I think we have to be careful. The world's changed in ways we don't understand. We can't just walk into the unknown and hope for the best. But we can't stay here forever either. We need to move, but we need to be smart about it."

Lydia nodded, her eyes filled with the same uncertainty that plagued them all. "And what about the tree? Do you think it's really gone?"

Isaac sighed. "I want to believe it is. But I keep feeling like... like something's still here. Like the tree's influence is too deep to just vanish. I don't know if we'll ever be free of it."

They fell silent again, listening to the ongoing debate among the survivors. Some were growing frustrated, eager to leave this cursed place behind. Others were more cautious, urging patience and planning. Isaac could feel the tension rising, the pressure to make a decision building as the hours dragged on.

Finally, it was **Vernon**, one of the last remaining researchers from the group that had studied the tree, who stood up to speak. His voice was soft but filled with the weariness of someone who had seen too much.

"The tree has left its mark on this world," he said, his eyes sweeping over the group. "But so have we. We've fought, we've survived, and we've won—for now. The world isn't the same as it was, but that doesn't mean we can't find a new way to live in it. We need to understand what's happened, yes. But we also need to keep moving forward. We can't stay here forever, but we can't rush blindly into the unknown either."

He paused, looking around at the faces of the survivors. "We're all that's left of the world we knew. Whatever comes next, we'll face it together."

Isaac nodded slowly, feeling a sense of agreement with Vernon's words. They had to keep going—cautiously, but with purpose. The world was broken, but they weren't. Not yet.

The Decision

By the end of the day, the survivors had reached a tentative decision. They would leave the ruins of the battlefield, but they wouldn't venture too far—at least, not yet. They needed time to regroup, to gather resources and information before deciding on their next steps. There was still too much uncertainty, too many unknowns about what the world had become.

As the sun began to set, Isaac and Lydia stood together, watching the horizon darken. The blood-red moon had faded, replaced by a thin sliver of the new moon that seemed almost fragile in the night sky.

"We'll find a way," Lydia said quietly, her voice filled with determination. "It's not over yet, Isaac."

Isaac nodded, though the uncertainty still gnawed at him. The tree was gone, but its legacy remained. And the future... the future was still a mystery.

But for now, they would keep going.

The New World

Isaac stood at the edge of the shattered battlefield, staring out at the ruins of the world that stretched before him. The sky was an eerie shade of pale gray, washed of color, with only faint streaks of pink from the fading blood-red moon still visible on the horizon. The ground was cracked and scarred, the deep gouges left by the tree's roots cutting jagged lines through the earth. But it wasn't just the land itself that had changed—there was something wrong with the air, with the very atmosphere that hung over everything.

It was as though reality itself had been warped by the tree's presence, leaving behind a world that felt unstable, uncertain. And in some places, the remnants of that corruption still lingered.

Isaac took a slow, deep breath, the weight of it settling heavily in his lungs. The survivors had made camp just beyond the wreckage of the battlefield, preparing to leave the area and venture into the unknown. But Isaac had felt compelled to explore the landscape around them before they moved on. He needed to see what had become of the world they had fought to save—needed to understand just how deep the tree's corruption had gone.

The land ahead of him was a wasteland of twisted, broken terrain. Trees had been uprooted and warped beyond recognition, their trunks split and gnarled like ancient, tortured hands reaching for the sky. The earth was uneven, with patches of ground that seemed to ripple and shimmer unnaturally, as if the fabric of reality itself was fraying at the edges.

Isaac stepped forward cautiously, his boots crunching over the cracked soil as he made his way into the heart of the destruction. His breath was steady, but his mind raced with the possibilities of what he might find. The tree was gone, but its influence… it was still here. He could feel it, like a dull pressure in the back of his mind, an ever-present reminder of the nightmare they had endured.

As he moved deeper into the ruined landscape, Isaac's eyes caught sight of something out of place. Just ahead, half-buried in the dirt, was the skeletal form of a creature—one of the **aberrations** that had once served the tree. Its many limbs were twisted at unnatural angles, its once glowing eyes now dull and lifeless. The aberration's body was partially decomposed, as though the life had been sucked out of it the moment the tree was destroyed.

Isaac knelt beside the creature, studying its grotesque form. Even in death, it was unsettling to look at. The aberrations had been born of the tree's dark power, twisted manifestations of the nightmare that had overtaken the world. Without the tree, they had withered, just like its roots, their connection to the corrupted energy severed. But the remnants of their presence—the remnants of the tree's influence—were still all around him.

As Isaac stood up, his gaze traveled to the distance, where he saw something that made his stomach turn. A patch of land about fifty yards away seemed to shimmer, the air above it warping as though the very fabric of reality was bending and distorting. It was subtle, barely noticeable at first, but as Isaac approached, the distortion became more apparent. The ground there seemed wrong, as though it wasn't fully real.

He stopped at the edge of the shimmering patch, unsure of what he was looking at. The air above the ground rippled like the surface of a disturbed pond, the light bending in strange ways. It was as though the world itself was struggling to hold itself together in that spot, as though the tree's influence had broken something fundamental. Isaac took a cautious step closer, his heart racing.

As he reached out, his hand hesitated at the edge of the distortion. His fingers brushed against the rippling air, and a jolt shot up his arm, like an electric shock. He pulled his hand back quickly, his pulse pounding in his ears. Whatever this was, it wasn't natural. It was a tear in reality—a remnant of the tree's power still lingering, warping the world even after the tree's destruction.

"Isaac!"

The voice startled him, pulling him out of his thoughts. He turned to see Lydia approaching, her expression tense as she navigated the uneven terrain. "We've been looking for you," she said as she reached his side. "What are you doing out here?"

Isaac gestured to the shimmering patch of air. "Look at this. It's like... reality is breaking apart. The tree might be gone, but whatever it did to the world, it's still here."

Lydia frowned, stepping closer to get a better look. She reached out cautiously, her hand stopping just short of the shimmering air. "I've seen something like this before, near the tree's roots after the first battle," she said, her voice low. "It's like the world's fabric is thin here, like the tree left wounds in reality itself."

Isaac nodded. "Exactly. I don't know how far this goes, or how many of these pockets there are, but it means the tree's influence hasn't fully disappeared. There are still pieces of it left behind, pieces that might never heal."

They stood in silence for a moment, both of them staring at the distortion with a mixture of fear and uncertainty. The tree had been destroyed, but its power had dug deep into the world, twisting it in ways they were only beginning to understand. Isaac wondered just how much of the world had been affected—how many of these broken places existed, waiting to be discovered.

"We have to be careful," Lydia said quietly, pulling her hand back. "We don't know what these distortions could do if we get too close. The tree may be gone, but the world isn't safe yet."

Isaac looked around at the ruined landscape, his eyes tracing the jagged lines of the cracked earth and the warped trees. The land felt dangerous, unpredictable, as though at any moment it could shift beneath their feet. And the thought of more aberrations, or something worse, rising from these pockets of instability made his skin crawl.

"You're right," Isaac agreed. "We can't take any chances. We need to warn the others about this. If we're going to survive in this new world, we need to understand what we're dealing with."

Lydia nodded. "There could be more of these distortions all over the place. Who knows what the tree did to the rest of the world."

The thought of an entire world filled with these warped, unstable patches made Isaac's heart sink. They had fought so hard to destroy the tree, but the consequences of its existence were still unfolding. It wasn't just about survival anymore—it was about understanding the new world they had been left with.

As they made their way back toward the camp, Isaac's mind raced with the possibilities of what they might face in the days and weeks to come. The tree's fall had been a moment of hope, but now, as they explored the wreckage, it was clear that their struggle was far from over. The world had been twisted by the tree's influence, and now they had to learn how to navigate a reality that no longer followed the rules they had once known.

The Camp and the Unknown

When Isaac and Lydia returned to the camp, they found the survivors in a subdued mood, their conversations quiet and their faces marked with the same uncertainty that Isaac felt. Vernon, one of the last remaining researchers, had gathered a small group of people around him, explaining what he had discovered about the lingering pockets of instability.

Isaac joined the group, listening as Vernon spoke in a low, serious voice. "The tree's roots reached deeper than we ever imagined. We've already found several patches of reality that seem… fractured, like the one Isaac and Lydia just saw. These areas are dangerous. We don't know how far the distortions go, or what could happen if we get too close."

A murmur of concern rippled through the group.

"We'll need to map these areas out," Vernon continued. "Avoid them if we can. But we also need to understand what's causing them, if we're going to have any hope of rebuilding."

Isaac's mind flashed back to the shimmering air, to the feeling of his hand brushing against the edge of the distortion. He wasn't sure what they could do about it—whether they could fix it, or if it was something they would just have to live with. But one thing was clear: the world they had known was gone, and this new world was one filled with dangers they hadn't yet fully grasped.

"We need to stay vigilant," Isaac said, stepping forward. "The tree may be gone, but its mark on the world remains. We're not safe yet, and we don't know how far these pockets of instability go. We have to be careful—and we have to be prepared for whatever comes next."

The survivors nodded, their faces grim but determined. They had fought hard to reach this point, but the journey wasn't over. The new world was filled with uncertainties, with remnants of the tree's dark power that would continue to challenge them.

And though Isaac wasn't sure what the future held, he knew one thing for certain: they would have to face it together, or not at all.

CHAPTER 35
The New Dawn or Eternal Night

The sky above the camp was a strange mixture of pale gray and deep red, the colors blending in a way that seemed almost unnatural. The blood-red moon, though dimmer now, still hovered ominously in the distance, its glow a constant reminder of the nightmare they had endured. It was a sight that, even after all the destruction, filled Isaac with a deep sense of unease. The tree was gone, its roots torn from the earth, but the world it had left behind still bore the scars of its influence. And Isaac couldn't help but wonder if they had truly escaped its grasp.

He stood on a small rise just outside the camp, looking out over the horizon. The landscape was barren, twisted by the tree's corruption. Patches of reality still shimmered in the distance, pockets of instability where the tree's influence lingered. The land itself seemed broken, fractured in ways that went beyond the physical. And though the survivors had begun making plans to move on, to rebuild, there was a part of Isaac that wasn't sure if that was even possible.

The past few days had been a blur of activity. The survivors had organized themselves into small groups, gathering what little supplies they had and discussing potential plans for the future. Some wanted to leave the area, to search for untouched land where they could start over. Others, like **Vernon**, believed they needed to stay and study the remnants of the tree's influence, to understand what had happened and how they might prevent it from ever happening again.

But Isaac? He wasn't sure where he stood. The weight of the battle, the loss of so many lives, the uncertainty of what came next—it all pressed down on him like a heavy stone, threatening to drag him into despair. He had fought so hard, had sacrificed so much, and now, standing on the edge of this new world, he wasn't sure if he had the strength to keep going.

He heard footsteps behind him, soft and measured. Lydia approached, her expression as tired as his own. She had been a constant presence since the tree had fallen, always there to offer support, to push him forward when he felt like giving up. But even she couldn't hide the exhaustion in her eyes, the toll that the battle had taken on her.

"You've been out here for a while," she said quietly, stopping beside him. "Are you okay?"

Isaac didn't answer immediately. He kept his gaze fixed on the horizon, watching as the light of the blood-red moon reflected off the shimmering patches of instability in the distance. "I don't know," he admitted, his voice heavy with uncertainty. "I don't know if any of us are okay."

Lydia sighed, following his gaze. "Yeah. I get that."

They stood in silence for a while, the wind brushing softly against their faces. Isaac could hear the faint sounds of the camp behind them—people talking, fires crackling, the occasional murmur of quiet laughter. It was strange, hearing those sounds in the wake of everything that had happened. It almost felt normal, as if the nightmare had ended and life was beginning to move on.

But Isaac knew better.

"Do you think we're really free of it?" he asked, his voice barely above a whisper. "The tree, I mean. Do you think it's really gone?"

Lydia didn't answer right away. She took a deep breath, her gaze distant. "I want to believe it is," she said finally. "We destroyed the core, we tore it from the ground. But I don't know, Isaac. This place… it still feels wrong. Like the tree left something behind. Like it's still out there, waiting."

Isaac nodded, his heart heavy. It was exactly what he had been feeling, that nagging sense that they hadn't truly escaped, that the tree's influence had burrowed so deeply into the world that it would never fully disappear. The blood-red moon, the fractured landscape, the pockets of instability—it all pointed to a world that was still very much under the tree's shadow, even if the tree itself was gone.

"So what do we do?" he asked, his voice tinged with frustration. "How do we rebuild in a world that's still broken?"

Lydia looked at him, her eyes filled with the same uncertainty that weighed on him. "We keep going. That's all we can do. We don't have the answers, but we can't stop. Not after everything we've been through. Maybe the world will never be what it was, but it's still our world. We have to try."

Isaac turned away from the horizon, his gaze drifting back toward the camp. The survivors were doing their best to move forward, to find some semblance of hope in the midst of the wreckage. But the question that gnawed at Isaac was whether it was enough. Could they rebuild? Could they create something new out of the ashes of a world that had been so thoroughly corrupted?

Or were they simply delaying the inevitable?

Lydia seemed to sense his inner turmoil. She placed a hand on his arm, her touch grounding him in the moment. "You've been carrying this weight for too long, Isaac. You led us through the worst of it, and now you're still trying to protect us. But you don't have to do it alone. We're all in this together."

Isaac looked at her, his heart aching with a mixture of gratitude and sadness. She was right, of course. He had taken on the burden of leadership, of responsibility, because he had believed that it was the only way to keep them all alive. But now, in the aftermath of the battle, that weight had become almost unbearable.

"I don't know if I'm ready for what comes next," Isaac confessed, his voice raw with emotion. "I don't know if I can do it."

Lydia smiled softly, though there was a sadness in her eyes. "None of us are ready. But that doesn't mean we stop. We take it one day at a time, one step at a time. And we face whatever comes together."

Isaac nodded, though the uncertainty still gnawed at him. He wanted to believe in Lydia's words, wanted to believe that they could rebuild, that there was a future waiting for them beyond the ruins. But the blood-red moon, still hanging in the sky like a watchful eye, made it impossible to shake the feeling that they hadn't truly escaped the nightmare.

The thought lingered in his mind, growing darker with each passing moment. What if the tree's influence wasn't just a physical presence? What if it had infected something deeper—something intangible, something that couldn't be destroyed with explosives or sorcery? What if the world itself had been changed, twisted beyond recognition?

What if the nightmare wasn't over?

Isaac took a deep breath, his gaze once again drawn to the shimmering patches of instability in the distance. He could feel the weight of the choice before him pressing down, a choice between hope and despair, between rebuilding and giving in to the fear that still gnawed at his soul.

Lydia's voice broke through his thoughts. "Isaac, we're not alone. As long as we have each other, we have a chance. Don't forget that."

Isaac nodded slowly, his mind still churning with doubt. He turned back toward the horizon, his eyes locked on the distant glow of the blood-red moon. Its light bathed the world in an eerie, haunting glow, casting long shadows over the landscape.

And in that moment, Isaac realized that he didn't have an answer. He didn't know if they were truly free, or if they had simply entered a new phase of darkness. The future was uncertain, a vast unknown filled with both hope and fear. They had survived the battle, but the war for the world's future was far from over.

Isaac took one last, long look at the moon, feeling the weight of everything they had lost and everything they still had to fight for. The choice hung in the air, unanswered.

And as the first light of dawn began to break over the horizon, casting a faint glow over the broken world, Isaac couldn't shake the feeling that the nightmare might not be over after all.

The End